Soft fingers touched his cheek. Hunter felt their touch all the way to his toes. It was like velvet against sandpaper.

"Thank you," she said.

"For what?" He was distracted by the hand warming his skin.

"For trusting me. For not assuming I'll mess it up."

Never had someone's words hit him so hard. Her words gave birth to a sensation like nothing Hunter had ever felt before. A primal sensation that rose from somewhere deep inside him, filling his chest and fueling his protectiveness.

Just like on that afternoon at the castle, everything disappeared from view but Abby's face. He felt as if he was falling, and grabbed the edge of the counter to stay balanced. His eyes dropped to her mouth. He wanted to kiss her again.

Dear Reader,

I love all my characters. Every once in a while, however, a character pops into my head whom I feel very protective of. Abby Gray is one of those characters. It was very important to me that she get not just a happy ending but the *right* happy ending—with the right man. Believe it or not, several auditioned for the role before Hunter Smith came along.

When Abby first sprang to life, I found myself with a spunky but downtrodden young woman just out of a horrendous relationship. I wanted to show how even smart women can get sucked into a spiral of insecurity and abuse. Getting out of that spiral isn't easy.

Fortunately Abby has Hunter to help her. Unfortunately Hunter has a few issues of his own when it comes to connecting with people. He'd much rather keep them at a distance to prevent himself from getting hurt. But, as happens with true heroes, Abby forces him to embrace his inner white knight. Before he knows what's happening, this sideline guy is involved in Abby's world and losing his heart!

Underneath all the romance there is an important lesson. That it's not enough simply to find a man who treats you right, but you must find yourself, as well. It's the lesson Abby needs to learn to get her happy ending. I hope as you're reading about Abby and Hunter's journey the lesson resonates with you, as well.

Thanks, as always, for reading my stories. I love writing them, and hope to entertain you for many more stories to come.

Best,

Barbara

BARBARA WALLACE

The Courage To Say Yes

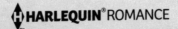

Recycling programs
for this product may
not exist in your area.

ISBN-13: 978-0-373-74255-4

THE COURAGE TO SAY YES

First North American Publication 2013

Copyright © 2013 by Barbara Wallace

Printed in U.S.A.

Award-winning author Barbara Wallace first sold to Harlequin® Romance in 2009. Since then her books have appeared throughout the world. She's the winner of RWA's Golden Heart Award, a two-time RT Book Reviews finalist for Best Harlequin Romance, and a winner of the New England Beanpot Award.

She currently lives in Massachusetts with her family. Readers can visit her at www.barbarawallace.com and find her on Facebook. She'd love to hear from you.

Recent books by Barbara Wallace

THE BILLIONAIRE'S FAIR LADY
MR. RIGHT, NEXT DOOR!
DARING TO DATE THE BOSS
THE HEART OF A HERO
BEAUTY AND THE BROODING BOSS
THE CINDERELLA BRIDE
MAGIC UNDER THE MISTLETOE

Other titles by Barbara Wallace available in ebook format.

To my boys Peter and Andrew—you are the best.

Thank you for your patience, your support, and your sacrifice.

CHAPTER ONE

"HEY, WHERE DO you think you're going?"

Pudgy fingers gripped Abby's wrist. She froze, hating herself for her reaction. "Let go of me, Warren," she said.

Her ex-boyfriend shook his head. "I'm not done talking to you."

Maybe not, but Abby was done listening. "There's nothing more to talk about." At least nothing she hadn't heard a dozen or three times before.

She tried to yank her arm free, but Warren held fast. "Since when do you tell me what to do?"

His fingers dug into the top of her wrist. He was going to leave a mark, dammit. "Warren, please." The plea slipped out from habit. "The customers…"

"Screw the customers." A couple heads turned in their direction. Abby didn't dare look to see if Guy, her boss, had heard, too.

"This is your fault, you know?" Warren told her. "I wouldn't have to come down to this—" he curled his upper lip "—this *diner* if you weren't being so childish."

As if his pouting and tantrums were the height of maturity. Abby knew better than to say anything. Hard to believe she'd once considered this man the answer to life's problems. Now he was the problem. One hundred ninety-five pounds of unshakable anger. Why couldn't he let her go? It'd been six weeks.

When it comes to us, I make the decisions, babe. Not you. That's what he always said.

How on earth was she going to get loose this time?

"Hey, Abby."

The sound of her name cut through the breakfast din, and made her pulse kick up yet another notch. Abby knew the speaker immediately. The photographer. She'd been waiting on him for the past dozen days. Always sat at the back corner table and read the paper, his expensive camera resting on the chair next to him. Quiet, hassle-free. Good tipper. Hunter something or other. Abby hadn't paid close attention. Whatever his last name, he was heading toward them, weaving his way through the tables with a graceful precision. Warren was not going to like the interruption.

"You want something?" he asked, before she could.

"I could use some more coffee." Hunter directed his answer to her as though her ex had never spoken. "That is, if you can pull yourself away from your conversation."

"Um…" She looked to Warren, gauging his reaction. After six years, she'd become an expert on reading his facial expressions. The telltale darkening of his eyes wasn't good. On the other hand, she knew he preferred discretion, choosing to do his bullying in private.

"You heard the man. He needs fresh coffee," Warren replied. "You don't want to keep your customers waiting."

Leaning forward, he placed a kiss on her cheek, a marking of territory, as much for her benefit as Hunter's. Abby had to fight the urge to wipe the feel of his mouth from her skin. "I'll see you later, babe."

His promise made her stomach churn.

"Nice guy," Hunter drawled from behind her shoulder.

"Yeah, he's a real peach."

She rubbed her aching wrist. What made her think she could walk away, and Warren wouldn't try to track her down? Just because he told her repeatedly that she was a worthless piece of trash didn't mean he was ready to give her up. As far as he was concerned, she was his property.

Warren's car pulled away from the curb. He was gone, but not for good. He'd be back. Later today. Tomorrow. A week from tomorrow. Ready to beg, scream, and try to drag her back home.

Oh, God, what if she wasn't in a public place when he returned? Or if he decided to do more than beg and scream? There were all sorts of stories in the news....

Her breakfast started to rise in her throat. She grabbed the chair in front of her.

"You okay?" she heard Hunter ask.

"F-fine." For the millionth time in six weeks, she pushed her nerves aside. Worrying would only mean Warren still had control. "I'm fine," she repeated. "I'll go get your coffee."

"Don't worry about it," he replied. "I'm good."

"But you said..." She stopped as the meaning of what he'd done dawned on her. He'd interrupted on purpose.

"You're welcome." Hunter turned and headed for his usual table.

Abby didn't know what to say. She should be grateful. After all, he'd just bailed her out of what could have become a very difficult situation. In all her years with Warren, no one had ever stepped up to help her before. On the other hand, she hadn't asked for his help. He'd just assumed she needed it, as though she were a helpless little victim.

Aren't you?

No. Not anymore. Despite what the situation looked like.

Oh, but she could just imagine what someone like the photographer thought, too. Her hand still shaking with nerves, she ran it through her hair before looking over at the back table. There sat Hunter, sipping the coffee he didn't need refilling. With his faded field jacket and his aviator sunglasses perched atop his thick brown hair, he looked exactly the way you'd picture a photographer. If you were casting a movie, that is. One where the daredevil photojournalist dodged bullets to get the shot. To be honest, his whole outfit— worn jeans, worn henley—would seem silly on anyone who didn't look like a movie star.

It didn't look silly on the Hunter. He had the cheekbones and complexion to rival any actor in New York City. Might as well throw Los Angeles in there as well, Abby decided. The build, too. Whereas Warren was soft and doughy, Hunter was hard, his body defined by angles and contours. Small wonder Warren had backed off. Her ex might be a bully, but he wasn't stupid. He knew when he was outclassed.

Too bad she couldn't get Warren to back off so easily.

"Abby, order up!" Guy stuck his craggy head out of the order window and slapped the bell. "Get your butt in gear. You want to stand around, you can go find a street corner."

As if this job was much better. She moved behind the counter to pick up the two plates of scrambled eggs and bacon Guy had shoved onto the shelf. "What about the home fries?"

Guy slapped a bowl of fried potatoes in front of her. "Next time, write it on the slip. And while you're at it, tell your boyfriend if he wants to visit, he can order like everyone else. I'm not paying you to stand around talking."

"He's not my— Never mind." She grabbed the potatoes, wincing a little at the pressure the extra plate put on her sore wrist. No sense arguing a losing point.

"Ignore him." Ellen, one of her fellow waitresses, said as she walked by. "He's like a bear with a sore head this morning."

What about the other mornings? "No change there then." Abby went to serve her customers before Guy blew another gasket.

Miserable as her boss might be, he was the only employer who'd been willing to hire an inexperienced waitress. Life with Warren hadn't left her with too many marketable skills, unless you counted walking on eggshells and knowing how to read bad moods. This job was the only thing keeping her from complete destitution. Without it, she might actually end up standing on a street corner.

Halfway through her rounds topping up customers' cups with fresh coffee, Abby felt the hair on the back of her neck began to rise. Someone was watching her. With more than the usual "trying to get the waitress's attention" stare. Automatically, her head whipped to the front door. Empty.

She didn't like being studied. In her experience, scrutiny led to one of three things: correction, punishment or a lecture. With a frown, she looked around the room until her eyes reached the back table where Hunter was sat. Sure enough, his attention was focused directly at her.

For the first time since she'd begun waiting on him, she took notice of his eyes. A weird hybrid of blue and gray, they looked almost like steel under the diner's fluorescent lighting. She'd never seen eyes that color. Nor had she been looked at with such… *Approval* wasn't the right word. It definitely wasn't the disapproval she was used to, either. She didn't know what to call it. Whatever the name, it caused a somersault sensation in the pit of her stomach.

Finally noticing he had her attention, Hunter nodded and held up his bill.

Abby's cheeks grew hot. Of course. Why else would he be looking for her other than to settle his bill? Warren's visit had her brain turned backward. After all, it wasn't as if she was the kind of woman who turned heads on a good day, let alone today. Her face was flushed and sweaty. And her hair? She'd given up trying with her hair hours ago.

She made a point of approaching his table on the fly, figuring she could grab his credit card and sweep on past, so as to avoid any awkward conversation. Considering his intervention earlier, she doubted there could be any other kind.

Unfortunately, as soon as she reached for the plastic, his grip on the card tightened.

"Is there a problem?" she asked when he wouldn't let go.

"You tell me." His eyes dropped to her wrist. To the bluish-red spots marked where Warren's fingers had been.

Dammit. She'd hoped there wouldn't be

any evidence. Letting go of the credit card, Abby pulled the cuff of her sleeve down to her knuckles. "I don't know what you're talking about."

"Do all your knishes look like eggs over easy?"

"What?" His question made no sense.

"The bill says I ordered blueberry knishes and rye toast."

"Sorry. I gave you the bill from two tables over by mistake."

"Again."

"Again," Abby repeated. That's right; she'd made the same mistake with him yesterday. She wondered if she'd messed up any other tables. Guy would kill her if she did. Again.

"Happens when you're distracted."

"Or busy," Abby countered, refusing to take the bait. She was trying to put Warren out of her head, and while she wasn't having much luck, talking about him wouldn't help.

Taking her order pad from her pocket, she flipped the pages. "Here's yours," she said, tearing out a new page. "Eggs over easy, bacon and whole-wheat toast. Same as every day. You want me to ring you up?" The sooner he settled his bill, the sooner he'd leave. Maybe then she could pretend the morning hadn't happened.

"Please."

Hunter noticed that this time when she reached for the card, she snatched it with her right hand, keeping her left still tucked inside her sweater. How hard did you have to squeeze someone's wrist to leave a bruise, anyway? Pretty damn hard, he imagined. A man had to have some serious anger issues to grab a woman that tightly.

Sipping the last of his cold coffee, he watched Abby ring up his bill, the sleeve of her sweater stretched almost to her fingertips. A poor attempt at hiding the evidence.

He'd known the minute the guy walked in that he was a first-class jerk. The overly expensive leather jacket and hair plugs screamed needy self-importance. It took him by surprise, though, when the jerk approached Abby. If anyone could be considered jerkdom's polar opposite, it was his waitress. Since his return stateside, Hunter had spent his meals at Guy's trying to figure out what it was that had him sitting in the same section day after day. Certainly wasn't the service, since Abby messed up his order on a regular basis.

Her looks? With her overly lean frame and angular features she wasn't what you'd call conventionally pretty. She was, however, eye-catching. Her butterscotch-colored topknot had a mind of its own, always flopping in one direction or another, with more and more strands working their way loose as the day progressed. The color reminded him of Sicilian beaches, warm and golden. Luckily, Guy was lax about health-code regulations. Be a shame to cover such a gorgeous color with an ugly hairnet.

She had fascinating eyes, too. Big brown eyes the size of dinner plates.

The bell over the front door rang. Hunter watched as she stiffened and cast a nervous look toward the entrance. Worried the jerk would return? Or that he wouldn't? Could be either. For all Hunter knew, his butterscotch-haired waitress had a big old dark side and liked being manhandled. Nothing surprised him anymore.

Well, almost nothing. He'd managed to surprise himself this morning. Since when did he step into other people's business?

A soft cough broke his thoughts. Looking up, he saw Abby standing there, coffeepot in her grip. Her right hand again. "Wrist sore?" he couldn't help asking.

"No." The answer came fast and defensively. "Why would it be?"

How about because she'd had the daylights squeezed out of it? "No reason."

If she wasn't interested in sharing, so be it. Wasn't his business, anyway. "Can I have a pen? For the receipt."

Her cheeks pinked slightly as she handed him the one from her pocket. Hunter scribbled his name and began gathering his belongings.

"Thank you." The words reached him as he was hanging his camera strap around his neck. Spoken softly and with her back turned, they could have been for the thirty percent tip. Or not. He saved them both the embarrassment of responding.

Distracted didn't begin to cover Abby's mental state for the rest of the day. She spent her entire shift expecting Warren to tap her on the shoulder. By the time she finished work, she'd managed to mess up four more orders. Not all the customers were as forgiving as Hunter, either. Guy was ready to run her out the door.

"Make sure your head's on straight tomorrow," he groused when she clocked out.

She wanted to tell him that if her head had ever been on straight, she wouldn't be working in a greasy spoon and dodging her ex.

Common sense kept her mouth shut. No need to make a bad situation worse by adding unemployment to the mix.

To her great relief, she stepped out to an empty street to wait for her taxi. Thank goodness. How she hated being back to looking over her shoulder. After six weeks, she'd foolishly begun thinking her life might actually be her own again. Granted, it wasn't the best of lives, but it was hers. Or rather, she'd thought so until Warren tracked her down. You'd think he'd be glad to be rid of her. Wasn't he forever telling her how she made his life so difficult?

Letting out a breath, she leaned against the railing in front of Guy's storefront. She hated taking a taxicab, too. Spending money earmarked for savings. It wasn't that she was so afraid of Warren. Sure, he'd gotten physical a few times—more than a few times—but she could handle him.

Liar. Why are you taking a cab then? Just a few hours ago, she'd worried today might the day he'd go over the edge.

Breaking up with Warren was supposed to be her new beginning. The end of walking on eggshells. Now she was stuck either leaving the one lousy job she could find, or praying that Warren had lost interest now that he'd tracked her down.

Angry tears rimmed her eyes. She sniffed them back. Warren wasn't going to win. She wouldn't let him.

Just then, movement caught the corner of her eye and she stiffened, hating herself even as she gripped the iron railing. Slowly, she pulled her thoughts back to her surroundings.

It was the photographer, coming down the street, camera slung around his neck. His sunglasses had migrated to his eyes, hiding their unique color. Didn't matter. He was still looking in her direction, his attention causing her stomach to quiver with unwanted awareness.

"Everything okay?" he asked as her taxi pulled up.

For crying out loud, couldn't a woman buy a moment of privacy? As it was, he already knew more of her business than necessary.

She slid into the backseat without answering.

Hunter spent the next day shooting landmarks around the city, updating his portfolio of stock photos. By this point he had more than enough shots for his files, but the project kept him busy. Downtime and he weren't good friends. Too much time off the job and he got antsy, a trait he'd inherited from his father. Inherited, or learned from watching. Either way, he hated being between jobs same as his father did. Only difference was Hunter didn't have a teenage son in tow.

It was midafternoon when he returned to his apartment building. One of the things he liked about this particular piece of real estate was that his street was basically an alleyway, meaning it had less crowds and traffic than other parts of the city. This time of day, the traffic was particularly slow. Guy's had closed, and rush hour had yet to begin.

As he rounded the corner, a familiar flash of butterscotch caught his eye. It was Abby, her angular frame bundled by a woolen coat. She was leaning against the diner's stair rail, her face and attention a thousand miles away. Her topknot, he noticed, had transformed itself. What was left of the mass had fallen to the nape of her neck, while most of the strands had worked loose and were framing her face.

Hunter felt a stirring deep in his gut, the sensation he got whenever he found a special shot. In Abby's case, the special element came from her posture. While she looked as exhausted as you'd expect a woman who'd spent eight hours on her feet would do, her shoulders and spine were ramrod straight. Pushing back against the weight of the world. Before she could notice his presence, he raised his camera and clicked off a half dozen frames. He managed to snap the last one as she turned, zooming in until her face filled the entire frame. That's when he saw the unshed tears that turned her eyes into shining brown mirrors. Hunter wondered if later, when he uploaded the shot, he'd see himself reflected in them.

He clicked one last photo and lowered the camera. Perfect timing, because she suddenly gripped the railing. She was still on edge from this morning, he realized. The reaction bothered him. He wasn't used to women growing rigid in his presence.

"Everything all right?" he asked, just as a taxicab pulled up alongside her.

He didn't expect an answer, and he wasn't disappointed. She slipped into the backseat without a word.

There was a padded shipping envelope propped atop his mailbox when Hunter finally entered his building—an advanced copy of a travel guide he'd shot earlier in the year. New Zealand, New Guinea; one of those places. He tossed the envelope, unopened, on his sofa. It landed with a puff of air, sending stray papers and a Chinese take-out menu sailing. Place had gone to pot since his assistant, Christina, had left to make her mediocre mark on the photography world. Not that she'd kept the place in great shape to begin with. She'd been far more interested in taking her photos than assisting him—a less than stellar characteristic in a photographer's assistant. At some point, he supposed, he should hire someone new and put this mess back in order. Unfortunately, like his last assistant, he was more interested in taking photos than in finding her replacement.

He thought about the pictures of Abby he'd just shot. He was eager to see how they'd turn out. If those eyes of hers were as riveting on paper as he suspected. When it came to photography, his instincts were rarely wrong. Then again, he'd learned through the lens of a master.

"No amount of raw talent can replace the perfect image," his father used to tell him. Joseph Smith had spent his life chasing the perfect photograph. Hell, he gave his life for the perfect shot. The rest of the world had to fall in line behind his work. A philosophy his son had learned the hard way how to embrace.

Sometimes, though, great images fell into your lap. Moving a pile of research books, he fired up the computer that doubled as his digital darkroom—one difference between his father's brand of photography and his. Modern technology made the job faster and easier. No makeshift darkrooms set up in hotels. All Hunter needed was a laptop and a memory card.

Though he had to admit that, every once in a while, he missed the old way. There was a familiarity to the smell of chemicals. As a teenager, he'd come to think of the smells as the one constant amid continual change. There were nights when he still walked into hotel rooms expecting the aroma to greet him.

Maybe he should install a darkroom in the building. Might make the place feel less like a way station.

Then again, building a darkroom was a lot like hiring an assistant. Nice in theory, but not as important as the photos themselves. Besides, nothing would make this apartment feel less like a way station because that's what it was. A place to sleep between assignments. No better than a hotel room, in reality. Less so, seeing how he actually spent more time in hotel rooms than his apartment.

Thumbnail images lined his computer screen. He'd shot more than he realized, a luxury of digital photography. He scrolled down until he found the series he'd taken of Abby. Sure enough, her face loomed from the screen like a silent-movie actress. The emotions bearing down on her reached out beyond the flat surface. He could feel the weariness. The grit, too. Hunter could see the glint of steely resolve lurking in the depths of her big, sad eyes.

To his surprise, he felt the stirring of arousal. A testimony to the quality of the shot. Good photos should evoke physical responses.

Of course, he didn't usually respond to his own work. He knew better than to get emotionally involved anymore. Start caring about the subject, and you set yourself up for problems. Images were illusory. The world on the other side of the lens wasn't as welcoming as photos made it appear. On the other side of the camera was pain, disinterest, loneliness, death.

Better to stay at a distance, heart safely tucked away where the world couldn't cause any damage. Of all the photography lessons his father had taught him, distance was the most important. Of course, at the time, he'd been too young to appreciate it, but eventually life had helped him to not just understand, but embrace the philosophy.

Yet for some reason, Hunter found himself

being drawn in by a simple photo of a waitress. Seduced by the emotion he saw lurking in her eyes. So much simmering beneath the surface…

Only for a moment, though. He blinked and the distance he prided himself on returned. He was once again the observer, and Abby's face merely another photograph. An intriguing, but ultimately meaningless, two-dimensional moment in time.

CHAPTER TWO

TO MOST NEW YORK residents, McKenzie House was nothing more than an inconspicuous brick row house with a faded green door. To the women inside, however, the house represented far more than an address. The rundown rooms meant a fresh start without abuse or domination. Abby was well aware that her story was mild in comparison to her roommates', but she was no less grateful. The gratitude rose in her chest once more as she fell back on the living area sofa. She was soon joined by Carmella, one of her fellow residents. "You look dead. Long day?"

"The longest. Warren showed up."

"What?" Carmella sat up like a shot. "He tracked you down? How?"

"I don't…"

Wait. Yes, she did. Oh, all the stupid…

"What?" Carmella asked.

"My mother. I called and gave her the diner's phone number in case of an emergency."

Abby grabbed her phone from her bag and punched the speed dial. Two rings and a harried female voice answered.

"Hey, Mom."

"Abby, um, hi! What a surprise." Joanne Gray sounded like she always did, as though looking over her shoulder. Which she probably was. "I can't really talk right now. I'm getting ready to put dinner on the table."

Abby checked her watch. By her calculations there was still ten minutes before the assigned dinnertime. "I'll only take a second, I promise. I was wondering if anyone's called the house looking for me."

"No one except your boyfriend, that is. He lost your new work number, and figured I knew it."

Mystery solved. "Mom, I told you Warren and I broke up."

Same way she had when Abby told her about the breakup, her mother disregarded the comment. "Warren explained how that was all a big misunderstanding."

"No. It was a breakup. I moved out of the apartment. Remember, I explained to you?" Along with the rest of the sordid story.

"I know what you said, honey, but I figured you'd changed your mind. Warren was so polite on the phone. And he's doing so well. You're lucky to have a man like that interested in taking you back."

Because that's what mattered. In Joanne Gray's eyes, a lousy man was better than no man at all. Didn't matter how miserable or mistreating—

"Joanne!" Abby's stepfather's bellow came through so loud she had to jerk the receiver from her ear. "What are you doing, talking on the phone?"

"I'm sorry," she heard her mother reply. "It's Abby. She had a question."

"She should know better than to call when it's dinnertime. Hang up. I'm hungry!"

There was some shuffling and her mother's voice came back online, a little more ragged than before. "I have to go, honey."

"Sure, Mom. I'll call soon."

Whether her mother heard the promise or not, Abby didn't know. She'd hung up, leaving her daughter on the line, with a headache and a sense of defeat. Some things weren't ever going to change. Not her mother. Not the way her mom viewed life.

"I was right," Abby said, letting the phone drop in her lap. "Warren called her."

Talk about ironic. When they lived to-

gether, Warren had no use for her parents.
Called them useless white trash. He'd spoken to her parents no more than three times
at most.

But of course, her mother would cave with
the phone number. Warren, salesman that he
was, would hardly break a sweat sweet-talk-
ing her.

Abby rubbed her suddenly aching head. "I
honestly thought that, after six weeks, he'd
move on."

"Well, some guys just don't like to give up
what they think is theirs."

Carmella should know. Her ex had torched
their apartment during a fight. Thankfully,
Warren never did more than twist Abby's arm
or deliver a swift backhand.

The silver bracelets lining Carmella's arm
shimmered against her dark skin as she pulled
back the curtain covering the window. "Any
chance he followed you?"

"No. He, um…left." Aided by a field jacket
and aviator sunglasses. "Hopefully, he got the
message and won't be back."

"Yeah, right. And I'm gonna be on the
cover of *Vogue* next week. You're kidding
yourself if you think he's giving up now that
he's tracked you down."

That's what she was afraid of, Abby thought,

rubbing her wrist. The marks had blossomed to full-blown bruises. Annoyance and shame rose in her throat. She was mad. Mad at Warren. Mad at her mother.

Most of all she was mad with herself for believing that living with him was the best she could ever do in life. For letting him take over her entire world, until she'd lost control and herself.

Well, no more. She'd rather be alone for the rest of her life than lose herself in a relationship again.

Why her mind drifted to Hunter at that moment, she didn't know. Correction. Hunter *Smith*. She'd read the name off his credit card. Now that she thought about it, she was mad with him, too.

A new emotion joined the others already warring inside her: embarrassment. She'd worked long and hard to escape Warren's clutches and start her new life. Last thing she needed was her action-hero customer thinking he knew her secrets. Or worse, sending her pitying looks with those steel-colored eyes of his.

It'd be too much to ask that he leave town by morning, wouldn't it?

Knowing her luck, he'd be back at his table tomorrow, with that field coat and those big broad shoulders. Checking the bruises on her wrist.

She'd rather face down her ex.

"Eggs over easy, wheat toast, side of bacon."

Abby held her order pad in front of her face like a shield. If she didn't look at Hunter's face, she wouldn't have to see his expression. Bad enough that the mere thought of facing him gave her stress dreams.

Given everything that had happened yesterday, she'd think Warren would be the one haunting her subconscious. But when she closed her eyes, it was Hunter who invaded her thoughts.

She knew why he was on her mind. It was because he knew her dirty little secret. For so long, keeping secrets was how she'd lived her life. Her mistakes—and man, did she make some whoppers—were hers to hide. To think that now someone else knew—saw—the evidence... Part of her wanted to crawl into a hole. Another part wanted to tell Hunter to take his sympathy and shove it. She settled for focusing on the two-by-three square in front of her face.

"You going to write the order down?" Hunter asked.

"Not necessary."

There was a long, drawn-out pause. "You sure?"

Against her better judgment, Abby lowered the pad to stare at him. "You don't think I can remember?"

"Did I say that?"

His silence said so for him. Granted, she'd forgotten a few orders in the beginning, but she'd improved a lot since then. "You've ordered the same thing for twelve days," she told him.

"Nice to know I'm so memorable."

More like predictable, she wanted to say. Though that wouldn't be quite true. She certainly hadn't predicted his behavior yesterday. "I'll go get your coffee."

"How's your wrist?"

Exactly the topic she hoped to avoid. "Fine," she replied in a stiff voice. Her fingers twitched with the urge to tug on her cardigan, to hide the gauze bandage peering out from beneath the cuff. The bruises were darker this morning. Dark enough that simply wearing long sleeves wouldn't be enough to hide them, so she'd covered them with a bandage. Her plan was to tell anyone who asked that she burned herself. Didn't it figure, the first person to say anything would be the one man she didn't want to hear from?

"I'll be back with your coffee," she said, turning on her heel.

Damned if she couldn't feel him watching her walk back to the counter. Awareness washed over her, making her insides quiver. She wasn't used to being looked at under any circumstances. In fact, Warren was the first man who'd ever paid her any kind of attention. Look how terrific that had turned out. Naturally, having a man as handsome as Hunter scrutinizing her set Abby's nerves on edge. Doubly so since she knew his scrutiny wasn't anything more than sympathetic curiosity. It made her feel like some wounded animal in the zoo. Out of the corner of her eye she caught her reflection in the stainless steel. Limp, uncooperative hair; pale skin. Yeah, like she'd attract attention. It scared her to think Warren was right. That he was the best she could do.

Good thing she didn't mind being alone.

Tugging her cuff down to her knuckles, she made her way back to Hunter's table.

"You're going to pull that sleeve out of shape," he remarked.

So what? It was her sweater. If she wanted to stretch it out, she would. "Do you need cream?"

"Don't tell me you forgot already?"

"Sorry. Guess you're not so memorable, after all." She reached into her apron pocket and removed the plastic creamer pods she'd grabbed when getting his coffee. The motion caused her sleeve to pull upward. Whether Hunter looked at the exposed bandage or not didn't matter; she felt he was and that was enough.

"I know what you're thinking," she said suddenly.

"You do?"

"Yeah." He thought he knew her story based on one short encounter. "You're wrong, though. I'm not."

"Not what?"

"Not..." She raised her bandaged arm. "Not anymore. I left Warren."

"Oh."

That was it? *Oh?* Abby watched him as he blew across the top of his cup, his lips pursing ever so slightly. It was the only change in his expression.

"Doesn't seem to be taking the breakup too well," he said finally.

"He'll adjust. Yesterday was..." No need getting into a long, drawn-out explanation. "Look, I'm only explaining because you—"

"Saw the bruises?"

"Say it a little louder, why don't you? They

didn't hear you downtown." Swiping at her bangs, Abby looked around at the other tables. Fortunately, no one had heard, or if they did, had decided not to share.

"I wanted to make sure you understood the deal. Because of yesterday. Not that I don't appreciate what you did and all."

"You're welcome."

Abby pursed her lips. "Point is, your help wasn't necessary. I have the situation under control."

"I could tell."

"Seriously, I do." She didn't like how his response sounded mocking. It made her even more defensive. Maybe she hadn't had control at that exact moment, but she would have handled the situation. "So you won't need to repeat the performance."

"In other words, mind my own business."

Exactly. "I'm saying it's not necessary."

Hunter nodded into the rim of his cup. "Good to know. I'm not really into rescues to begin with."

"You're not?" Could have fooled her.

"Nah. Like you said, it's not my business."

"Then why…?"

"Did I step in yesterday?" He shrugged. "What can I say? My mother was a Southerner and raised me to be a gentleman."

So he was protecting her honor? Abby's stomach fluttered. "Well, you can tell your mother the lesson sank in."

"I would, but she's dead."

"Oh. I'm sorry."

He shrugged again. "Don't be. It was twenty years ago."

When he was a kid. The action hero had a sad past. A human side to balance the movie star exterior. Her edge toward him softened a little.

"Abby! Customers!" Guy's voice cut over the clanging of plates and silverware. "Stick and move, will ya?"

"Duty calls." Any more conversation would have to wait. "I'll be back with your eggs soon as they're ready."

Under control, huh? Hunter watched as she bustled off to wait on two businessmen seated two tables over, her knotted ponytail bouncing in cadence with her steps. The gauze on her wrist flashed white as she raised her order pad. Who was she trying to convince with that statement? Him or herself?

Not his business. The lady said she had the situation under control. He was off the hook.

Which suited him fine. Besides, he thought as he raised his coffee mug, maybe the lady did have the situation under control, and that air of vulnerability was all in his head. Wouldn't be the first time.

He reached into his messenger bag and pulled out a manila folder. Probably not the best way to keep the dark thoughts at bay, but he looked at the photo anyway. It was the picture he'd taken of Abby. After much deliberation, he'd decided to print the photo in black-and-white, finding the absence of color highlighted the shadows on her cheeks.

Hunter stared at her eyes. There it was. The sadness. They always said eyes were the windows of the soul and that photography captured a little slice of that spirit. In Abby's case, her spirit was wrapped in a kaleidoscope of emotions. Question was, what emotions were they? Photography, like all art, was open to interpretation. What looked soulful could really be distant, simmering resentment waiting to blow up in your face.

Another argument for focusing on simply taking the picture.

Finished with the businessmen, Abby had moved back to the order window, where she was now dancing back and forth with another waitress who was laden with plates. Hunter let his eyes skim Abby's figure. The misshapen cardigans she wore every day didn't do her silhouette any favors. She had great legs, though. They managed to look shapely despite the sensible shoes. He tried to imagine what they'd look like with her in a shorter skirt and high heels. Not bad, he bet.

He was still contemplating when Abby set a plate in front of him. "What's this?" she asked.

She'd spotted the photo. Since the subject was self-explanatory, he took a bite of his eggs before answering. "You."

"I know it's me. When did you take it?"

"Yesterday. Right here on the sidewalk."

Her brows drew together. "How? Were you following me?"

"Don't be ridiculous." Although given her ex, he could see how she might jump to that conclusion. "I live across the street. I took the photo on my way back to my building."

"Without saying anything?"

"Alerting you to my presence would have spoiled the shot."

"So instead, you creeped."

Hunter set down his fork. "I was discreet. It's what a good photographer does."

"Is it now?" Shooting him a dubious look, she wiped her hands on her apron and picked up the photo.

"Wow," she said after a minute.

Exactly his reaction when he'd finished the digital enhancement. Hunter didn't usually care about compliments; he had enough confidence in his skills that other opinions didn't affect him. But hearing Abby's whispered surprise, and seeing the look of genuine wonder that accompanied it, set off an eruption of heated satisfaction.

"I look…" As she paused to find the word, she worried her upper lip between her teeth. It was such an expressive gesture, Hunter had to fight the urge to grab his camera and snap away.

At last she set the photo down. "Tired," she said. "I look tired."

"Yeah, you do." No sense lying when there were such pronounced circles under her eyes. "But I think you're missing the point." The weariness was part of what made her—that is, her picture—so captivating. "The photo is telling the story."

"What? Woman works hard for the money? Donna Summer already covered it."

"Very funny."

"I'm here all week." Her mood sobered as she brushed her fingertips along the glossy paper. "Sadly, this might be the best picture I've ever had taken."

"Not surprising. It's probably the first time you were shot by a quality photographer."

She laughed. A short, sweet laugh that turned her features bright. To Hunter's surprise, seeing her face light up sent the heat in his gut six inches lower. "Wish I'd known. Might have saved me from years of awful holiday photos. Warren said I looked like a deer about to be plowed into."

"Were you?" Hunter asked. "About to be run over?"

Brown eyes raised to look at him. "I thought you said the problem was the photographer."

"Photographers also capture reality."

"Doesn't that just support my argument about looking terrible?"

"Only if you're terrible-looking to begin with."

"Generally speaking, of course." Pink colored her cheeks and she looked at the floor. It made him wonder how often she heard compliments. Considering her d-bag of an ex-boyfriend, it likely wasn't often.

Hunter handed her the photograph. "Here."

"You're giving it to me?"

"Why not? It's a picture of you."

"Yeah, but..." Whatever she was going to say drifted off as her hand brushed against his. Hunter watched as her eyes widened at the contact. Fear of another man's touch? Her pupils were wide and dark, turning her irises into thin, brown frames.

For some reason, he found himself wanting to extend the contact, and so he dragged his index finger slowly across the back of her hand as he withdrew. Beneath his touch, he felt her skin quiver.

"Thank you," she whispered.

"You're welcome."

"So *this* is how you take care of your customers."

Warren. Abby yanked her hand away, sending the picture fluttering to the ground. Before either she or Hunter could move, her ex-boyfriend leaned over and picked it up. Abby tried to snatch it from his grip, but he held tight. "Nice picture. You look…good."

Abby couldn't answer. Her insides were too tense. Across the way, she could see Guy watching them. *Please don't let there be trouble.* "I thought I told you yesterday that I didn't want to see you."

"That was yesterday. I figured now that you had time to sleep on things, you'd changed your mind. Course, that was before I realized why you didn't want me around."

Warren's eyes were hard and glittered like diamonds. Abby knew the look well. His calm demeanor was an act, a respite before the storm.

Hadn't she told Hunter she had the situation under control? She squared her shoulders. "Warren, you need to leave."

"Not until we talk. You changed your phone number."

"That should have been a clue that I don't want to talk with you."

"Come on, babe, stop being stubborn. I know I messed up, but that's no reason to run away. Let's get out of here and talk. You'll see how sorry I am, and you'll change your mind."

No way. "I'm not going anywhere with you," she told him.

"There you go, being stubborn again."

He moved to grab her hand. Abby jerked out of his grasp. "Oh, sure, I can't touch you, but you got no problem letting him paw you," he snarled.

"She said she didn't want to talk with you."

Great. Until then, Hunter had been quiet. What happened to staying on the sidelines? "I've got this, Hunter," she told him. Last thing she needed was for him to butt in and make a bad situation worse.

Warren's mottled face grew a shade redder. "'This'?" Too late, Abby realized her poor choice words. The switch flipped and the true Warren appeared. "You think I'm something you need to 'handle'?"

"That's not what I meant."

"I know what you meant, you ungrateful cow." This time when he reached for her, he was successful, latching on to her arm with an iron grip. "I'm done playing around. Let's go."

She stood her ground. "No."

Warren yanked her arm. Abby winced.

"The lady said no." Hunter had gotten up and moved between them, essentially blocking their exit.

"Get out of my way," Warren said.

"How about you let go of her arm?"

By now the other customers were watching. Guy had come out from the kitchen and was about two seconds away from throwing them all out. Abby's pulse began to race. She half considered going, if to only keep the scene from escalating any further.

"We can talk," she said, scrambling for a compromise. "But here. Sit down and I'll bring you some coffee."

It didn't work. "Since when do you tell me what I can and can't do? After everything I've done for you? You're lucky I'm taking you back after the way you humiliated me."

"I'm not going back!" For crying out loud, it was like a broken record. Abby yanked herself free, only to stumble backward into Hunter's table, knocking his coffee cup off balance. The cup fell on its side, hot liquid spilling over the edge, where it dripped on the camera below.

"Son of a—" Hunter grabbed for it just as the liquid began running down the outer casing. "This is a five-thousand-dollar camera."

"Serves you right for butting in where you don't belong." Warren sneered.

Hunter set the camera down on a clean table. "That so?" he asked. His voice was low and precise. Compared with Warren's bluster, the quiet deliberateness sounded like ice. The air in the diner chilled.

"Seems to me," Hunter said, stepping into the other man's space, "that the problem started when you walked in the door. Now if my camera has any damage at all, you're going to pay."

Her ex-boyfriend scoffed, not realizing he was out of his league. "I'm not paying you for anything."

Hunter took another step. "Oh, I think you will."

"Okay, you three…"

A standoff. Just great. It figured Warren

would choose today to become macho and proud. It was the money. He would run into a burning building to protect five thousand dollars. Meanwhile, Guy was limping over to them. Abby almost groaned out loud. This could only end one way. Badly and with her getting fired. Quickly she stepped between the two men, hoping to regain control before Guy took action. "Look, guys, I'm sure if there's a problem we can—"

"Stay out of this!" Warren snapped. With that, he did what he did best—shoved her aside. Stuck between two tables, Abby found herself with little room to maneuver. Her feet tangled with a chair leg and she fell to the floor, but not before her back slammed into the edge of one of the tables. The table tipped, scraping her skin from bra strap to waist, and sending its contents spilling. Glass and silverware landed on the floor behind her.

So did Hunter's camera. It hit the floor with a crack. The diner went still.

After that, everything happened in a flash. A patron gasped, Guy started yelling, and Abby barely had time to catch her breath before Hunter's fist connected with Warren's jaw.

"Still think you have the situation under control?" Hunter asked.

The two of them sat on a marble bench in the corridor of the new courthouse. After Hunter threw his punch, and Guy threw the three of them out on the sidewalk, Warren had insisted on dragging a nearby traffic cop into the mess by claiming he'd been assaulted. All three of them had ended up in a police station, where Hunter, ever helpful, had suggested the police ask about the bruises on Abby's wrist. They did, and after a whole lot of questions, she found herself here, at the courthouse, waiting to speak to a judge about a nonharassment order against Warren.

"No," she said, answering Hunter's question. She felt anything but in control. Though she might have been if he'd minded his own business. "I could have sworn I told you to mind your own business."

"You'd rather I let him twist your arm off?"

What she'd rather was if the whole incident had never happened. "You didn't hit him for me," she pointed out.

"No, I hit him because he damn near destroyed my camera. And because he shoved you to the ground."

"Yeah, let's not forget that," Abby replied, arching her back. No sense pointing out she was the one, technically, who'd knocked over the camera. Nor the fact that the camera wouldn't have fallen in the first place had he minded his own business—as he claimed he preferred to do.

Letting out a frustrated sigh, she looked down at Hunter's hands. They were big, strong hands, she noted. Showing barely a mark where his fist had connected with Warren's face. "You get most of the ink off?" she asked.

His shoulder moved up and down. "Most of it."

That was another thing. Because Warren had cried assault, Hunter had found himself being charged. Good thing her knight in shining armor didn't have any outstanding warrants, or they might still be at the station house. Abby supposed she should feel bad about the fingerprinting and all, but again, it wouldn't have happened if he hadn't interfered. In fact, if he hadn't interfered the day before, none of today would have happened at all.

She let out another sigh. "Do me a favor. Next time I say I've got a situation handled, stay out of it. I don't care what your Southern mother taught you."

"Do I have to remind you that saying you could handle the situation caused part of the problem? Unless your idea of handling was to get dragged out into the street. 'Cause that's where your ex-boyfriend was taking you."

Recalling Warren's grip on her arm, Abby winced. Hunter was right, unfortunately. She just couldn't bring herself to say thank-you. Not quite yet. "Well, after I meet with the judge, I won't have to worry about Warren bothering me again. Nothing says 'we're over' like a restraining order."

"I'm surprised you didn't get a court order before," Hunter remarked.

"I didn't think I'd need one." A stupid assumption now that she thought about it. She should have listened to the ladies at McKenzie House. They'd told her Warren wouldn't let her end things on her terms.

Why weren't courthouse benches made more comfortable? The narrow space forced Abby and Hunter close together. Well, that and the fact that his long frame took up so much space. His thigh was pressed against hers and she could feel his jacket brush against her sleeve every time he breathed. The increased body heat had her feeling off balance. She tried shifting her weight, but nothing changed. Everywhere she moved, Hunter was there, his hard, lean body pressed tightly against hers, the contact sending disconcerting tingles up and down her arm.

This was crazy. She was in a courthouse, for goodness' sake, filing a restraining order. Wrapping her cardigan tightly about her, she stood up, only to wince when her clothing rubbed her bruised skin.

"How is your back?" Hunter asked.

The truth? Her back stung like heck every time she moved, and a headache pounded her temples. "I've had worse."

"You always such a bad liar?"

Abby looked at him through narrowed eyes. "What can I say? I'm off my game."

And who could blame her? Too much had happened in a very short time. Her system needed recharging. She crossed the hallway to lean against the wall, grateful for the additional personal space.

Hunter stayed on the bench, forearms resting on his knees. Abby had been too annoyed with him earlier to notice, but he looked as tired as she felt. "Why are you still here?" she asked, voicing a question that had been bothering her for a while. "The police said you could go a couple hours ago."

"I've stayed this long. Might as well see the process through."

Thus making a difficult situation all the much more awkward. Abby combed her fingers through the hair around her face. "I thought you weren't into rescues."

"I'm not. But I'm also not into leaving loose ends."

"That's how you see me? As a loose end?"

"Your goon of an ex-boyfriend is," he replied. "What on earth were you doing with him, anyway?"

Something she'd asked herself a million times, hating the answer. "He was different when we met. Bought me gifts. Took me places. I bought the act." She could feel Hunter's eyes on her, waiting for more. "You've got to understand. I wasn't used to nice.

"Or attention," she added, fiddling with a button. "I mean, he lost his temper once in a while, but he was always really sorry. Wasn't all that different from other families, right?"

Hunter raised a brow.

"I was nineteen years old. What did I know?" Obviously not a lot.

What bothered her the most about her story was how easily she'd made Warren the center of her world. Everything these past years had been about him. His moods, his wishes. Letting herself disappear. That was her biggest crime. All because he'd been nice.

"Sounds pretty stupid, huh?" she said to

Hunter, although she could have easily been talking to herself.

Her companion hadn't changed his position other than to lower his gaze to the floor. She wished she could see his eyes, to know what he was thinking. How could someone like him ever truly understand? A man who looked like Hunter, who carried himself with as much confidence as Hunter—his world was probably filled with men and women begging for his company. What would he know about "falling for a kind word"?

"I try to make a point of not judging," he said as he studied the palm of his hand.

"Really? I think you might be the first."

Though his eyes remained focused on the ground, Abby saw his cheek tug in a smirk. "Let's say I've learned not to make assumptions about things. Or people."

"Bad experience?"

He looked up and it shocked her to see how closed off his face had become. As if a steel curtain had dropped over his eyes. "You could say that."

Abby knew the terse tone of voice. He didn't want to elaborate. Apparently, she was the only one who was required to share.

"Anyway," she said, "eventually I came to my senses, and one day while he was at work,

I took off with three months' worth of grocery money." There was more to the story, of course. Much more. Situations like hers didn't blossom overnight. But she'd said enough to make her point. Hunter wasn't the only one who could refuse to elaborate. "Never thought I'd be sitting here, though."

All right, technically standing. She pulled her sweater tighter. The thing had been tugged at so much she was amazed it had any shape left. She was tired. The day's events were finally catching up with her, pressing down with an unbearable weight.

"Do you still love him?"

"Good Lord, no," she replied, surprised at how emphatic she sounded. "Those feelings died a long time ago." Sometimes she couldn't believe she'd once cared for the man. "Tell you one thing," she said, toeing the marble floor. "Six years ago I never would have believed I'd end up here."

"That, sweetheart, makes two of us."

The courtroom door opened, preventing Abby from commenting. "They're ready for you, Miss Gray," the uniformed woman said.

This was it. Abby looked to Hunter, hoping for what, she didn't know. "Time to get Warren out of my life once and for all," she said, forcing a determined note into her voice. It wasn't until she reached the courtroom door that she added under her breath, "I'm just sorry I have to be here."

Me, too, thought Hunter as he followed her into the courtroom. There were a thousand better ways he could be spending his day.

She was right; he didn't have to be here. So why was he? Why on earth had he spent two extra hours sitting on hard marble benches and watching some woman he barely knew fill out forms?

Maybe because you're the reason she's here in the first place. If he hadn't thrown the first punch—the only punch—Warren would never have gone wailing to the police. But that camera was Hunter's baby, dammit! What was he supposed to do? Just let the jerk damage it?

Yeah, because Hunter's outburst was all about photography equipment, and had nothing to do with seeing Abby fall backward. He could try to sell himself that excuse all day long. Truth was, he hadn't gone after Warren until she'd lost her balance. Then Hunter had seen red.

What the hell was wrong with him? His job was to capture action on film, not become the action. Yet here he was, playing hero two days in a row. Civilized society be damned.

After dragging all afternoon, the process in front of the judge moved quickly. Hunter had to give Abby credit. It couldn't be easy answering the same questions over and over. Although he could tell from her posture that she was wound tighter than tight, the only outward sign of stress were the fingers fidgeting with the hem of her sweater. He found himself wanting to snatch them up and hold them still.

It took less than ten minutes for the judge to approve her petition and grant a temporary order. A member of the sheriff's department would serve Warren that night. Hunter didn't miss the way Abby's shoulders relaxed at the announcement.

"Congratulations," he said when he met her at the door.

"You make it sound like I won the lottery."

"You got rid of the ex."

She seemed far from relieved. Surely she didn't regret the order?

"Don't be ridiculous," she snapped, giving him a dirty look when he asked. "It's just…" She swiped at her bangs. "I feel like an idiot for buying his act."

"Happens to the best of us."

She glanced at Hunter sideways. "Meaning it happened to you?"

"Meaning you're probably not the only one Warren fooled." The elevator doors opened and they stepped inside, Hunter immediately making his way to the rear. Truth was, he understood what had happened to Abby all too well.

Shoving bad memories back where they belonged, he continued. "If it's any consolation, I know his type. Faced with a real obstacle, he'll back off. Fifteen days from now, he'll have moved on to someone else."

"In other words, some other woman gets suckered and goes through what I went through. Lucky her."

Hunter didn't know how to reply.

They rode down the three floors in silence. It had been a long day. Stealing a look in Abby's direction, Hunter regretted packing his camera away. She wouldn't want to hear it, but her appearance at that moment told a real story. With the fluorescent light casting a gray pall on her skin, he could see the cracks in her stoicism. The pronounced circles under her eyes, the subtle slump of her shoulders. Her makeup had worn off hours earlier and her hair… Her hair was an all-out mess. The morning's haphazard ponytail was now an out-of-control bunch. Most of the strands had fallen loose, and those that hadn't weren't far behind. Made him wonder if her insides weren't in a similar state.

And, strangely enough, wonder if she could use a hug.

When they stepped outside, shadows were crawling up the sides of buildings, engulfing the lower halves of high-rises in shade. Sunset came early this time of year. In a few hours, the streets would be dark. So much for taking any pictures. His flash and lighting equipment were back at the loft.

"What are you going to do now?" he asked Abby. "Head home?"

Asking only reminded him that he knew very little about her life beyond the diner. Did she have a home? She'd said she'd left with only a few months of grocery money. What kind of apartment did that get a person? He was embarrassed to realize he didn't know.

"Actually, I thought I'd go back to the diner. I need to talk to Guy about my job. If I still have one," she added in a low voice.

"I'm sure once you explain the situation…"

From the look she shot him, Abby didn't believe that possibility any more than he did.

"Sure, he'll understand. Because Guy's such an understanding person. I bet when he yelled 'get out and stay out,' he was only kidding."

Unfortunately, she was probably right; her job was history. Hunter felt a little bad about that.

A cab pulled to the curb. He beat Abby to the rear door, opening it and motioning for her to climb into the backseat. "We're going in the same direction. No sense grabbing separate taxis."

"True." Despite sounding less than thrilled, she slid across the leather seat, only to stop halfway across. Holy Mother of— Had she been hiding those legs under that ugly skirt all this time? Her uniform had bunched up, revealing a pair of creamy white thighs. "One thing," she said. "On the off chance I convince Guy to let me keep my job, there's something I'd like you to do."

"Sure." Still blown away from the legs, Hunter was more than glad to let her talk. Especially if it kept the view from disappearing. "Just name it." He forced himself to look her in the eye.

The gaze that met his was hot and frosty at the same time. "Find somewhere else to eat."

CHAPTER THREE

"GET OUT."

Abby looked over her shoulder, hoping Guy was talking to Hunter and not to her. Apparently her request in the cab had fallen on deaf ears, because the photographer had insisted on following her inside after the cab ride home.

Her plan had been simple. Catch Guy before he locked up, apologize and assure him that Warren wouldn't be back. If necessary, beg and plead a little. Instead, she barely got through the door when he came around to the front of the counter. Dish towel slung over his shoulder, he jabbed the air with his gnarled finger. "Both of you," he said. "Out."

Abby almost went. After all, six years of being pliant didn't disappear overnight. Taking a deep breath, she held her ground. "Can't we talk about this?"

"There's nothing to talk about. I told you

when I hired you to keep your drama outside, and I meant it. You can't do that, you're out of here. There are plenty of waitresses who can do your job and who won't cause fist fights during my breakfast rush."

"Abby didn't cause the fight."

"Stay out of this," she snapped to Hunter. His help had caused enough problems.

"Fine." He raised his hands in mock surrender. "You're on your own."

"Thank you." Too bad he hadn't backed off so readily this morning.

"Can't you give me another chance?" she asked, turning her attention back to her boss. Her ex-boss. Hopefully soon to be boss again. "I know this morning was bad."

Guy waggled his index finger again. "Not only did you cause a fight, you left us short-handed."

"I know, and I'm really, really sorry. I promise to make it up to you."

"Who's gonna make it up to the customers I lost?"

It was a neighborhood restaurant with regular customers. He hadn't lost anybody. Telling him he was exaggerating wouldn't help her cause, though. If she'd learned anything from her years with Warren, it was when to keep her comments to herself. Instead, she moved to the second half of her plan. "Please, Guy. I'm begging you. I really need this job."

"You should have thought about that before bringing your little love triangle to work."

Love triangle? That's what he thought today was about? A love triangle?

"That is definitely not what happened," she said.

Guy dismissed her with a slap of his towel from one shoulder to another. "Don't care what it is," he said. "You're still gone." He turned his back.

Gone. As in fired. She couldn't be. "But Warren won't be back," she said, chasing after him. "I went to court. I got a restraining order."

The kitchen door swung shut in her face. "You still owe me a paycheck!" she hollered through the order window.

"What paycheck? I'm keeping it to cover the damages."

Damages, her foot. A couple broken dishes wouldn't take a whole paycheck, even with Guy's cheap wages.

Could this day get any worse?

"Come back tomorrow after he's calmed down," she heard Hunter say.

What good would that do? Guy wasn't going to change overnight. Why was Hunter still here, anyway? "Don't you have pictures to take or something?" she asked him. She would have thought he'd be on his way a long time ago.

"Lost all the good light," he replied.

"Oh, good. Then we've both lost something. I feel so much better." Rude? Yes, but she wasn't in the mood to be pleasant. Pushing her way past him, she headed to the front door. As if he had all day, Hunter accompanied her.

"You'll find another job, you know."

Easy for him to say. He had a job. "Do you have any idea how hard it was to get this one?" Of course he didn't. "News flash. Jobs don't grow on trees. Especially when you don't have skills. Or experience." Only thing she knew how to do was cook, clean and manage Warren's tantrums. Hardly stuff to build a résumé on.

"Thanks to today, I can't even use Guy as a reference."

Suddenly exhausted, she sank down on the steps of the building next door. Her body felt as if it'd been hit by a truck. Come to think of it, she might be better off if she had been hit by a truck. At least then she'd be in a hospital bed, and Guy might feel bad enough to let her keep her job.

She jammed her fingers through her hair, destroying what was left of her ponytail. "You know what really stinks?" she asked Hunter. "Warren's the bad guy in all of this and he's got everything. The apartment, a job, money—"

"A shiny new restraining order."

"Big whoop. So he can't come within a hundred yards. You said yourself, he'll move on before the hearing. Meanwhile, what do I have? No job and nine hundred lousy dollars in the bank. You tell me where that's fair."

"I can't."

Tears burned the back of her eyes. She blinked them away. Very least she would do was keep her pride. "All I wanted was to get my life back. Is that so freaking wrong?"

"No."

"I was close, too." She was. She had a job. She was saving money. Until Mr. Action Hero decided to live up to his looks. Now everything was ruined. "Why'd you have to punch him?"

Hunter sat on the step next to her. "I already told you."

"I know, I know. He almost broke your fancy-schmancy camera."

"That fancy-schmancy camera, as you put it, happens to be my life."

"So was my job!" Abby flung the words back at him. "Bet you didn't think about that when you decided to get all tough with Warren, did you? Who cares about Abby, right? Not like she matters. She's just some useless piece of…"

The dam broke and all the frustration that had been building since the morning came roaring free. She was angry. At Hunter. At Warren. Mostly, though, at herself for letting herself be held down for six long years and ending up here in the first place. With hot tears threatening to blind her yet again, she lashed out at the first thing she could reach, which happened to be Hunter's chest. "Damn you," she said, slapping at his jacket. "Damn you, damn you, damn you."

A pair of arms reached around her body, reining in her blows. *Not on your life,* she thought. She wasn't going to let him trap her and force her to stop. No one was going to force her ever again. Blind slaps became shoves. "Let me go."

He didn't. Nor did his grip grow harsh, as she expected. He simply held her in a firm but gentle embrace while she shoved and slapped until she didn't have any struggle left. Worn-out, she collapsed against his chest. Sometime during her tirade, the tears had escaped;

she could feel the cotton beneath her cheek growing damp.

Eventually her breathing slowed and Abby became aware of the heartbeat beneath her ear. Closing her eyes, she listened to its slow, steady thump, letting the cadence calm her own racing pulse. Hunter's clothes smelled faintly of detergent and fresh wood. As she inhaled, letting the scent fill her nostrils, it dawned on her that she'd never been held like this before. Without anger or ulterior motive. The experience was comforting and unsettling at the same time.

"Let me go," she muttered one more time into the folds of his jacket.

"Depends. Are you done?"

"I'm fine."

"I didn't ask if you were fine. I asked if you were done."

Abby let out a sigh. "I'm fine and I'm done. Better?"

Hunter's answer was to release her. Abby shivered at the abrupt departure, the way a person did when having the covers ripped from them while sleeping. The warmth she'd been feeling disappeared into the autumn night.

"I don't like being restrained," she told him, hugging her body.

"I don't like being slapped."

As if she could do damage to a body as firm as his. "Sorry. Been a long day."

She could feel his gaze on the top of her head. The sensation made her want to squirm, and she had to stare at the top button of his shirt to keep from doing so.

"Come on," he said finally.

That made her look up. "Come where?"

"I haven't eaten since breakfast and I'm starved," he said, as if that would explain everything. "Judging from your meltdown, I'm guessing you could use some food, too."

"I'm not hungry."

"Again, I didn't ask if you were hungry, I said you probably needed food."

"So?"

"So, there's an Indian restaurant around the corner."

"You're asking me out?" The hair on the back of her neck stood up.

"I'm offering to buy you something to eat. You coming?"

Everything she'd ever experienced in life told her to say no. Despite spending the day with her, Hunter Smith was a stranger, and by going anywhere alone with him, she'd only be buying trouble. After all, everything came with strings attached. Lord knew what kind of strings Hunter Smith wanted.

"Why?" she asked, swiping at her damp cheeks. "What's the catch?"

"No catch."

So he said. Last thing she needed was a man thinking he could take over her life. "Because if this is some kind of come-on, you can forget it. No matter what you think, I'm not an easy—"

"No catch," he repeated, a little more emphatically this time. "I want to eat. I'm offering you a chance to eat, too. You can come with me or you can stand out here until Guy tosses you off the sidewalk. Your choice."

Hunter stepped off the curb. "And by the way, as far as easy is concerned? You've got way too much baggage to ever be easy."

Damn straight she did. Abby considered the broad shoulders walking away from her, deliberately not thinking about how good it had felt when she'd rested her body against him. What she did think about was how her head felt as if it were about to explode. As much as she hated to admit it, having food in her stomach would help. Free food would help even more, given her return to unemployment.

"Fine. But you're paying." She stepped off the curb to join him.

For a dinner with no catch, Hunter certainly picked a fancy-enough restaurant. Abby looked around at the rust-colored walls and copper fixtures. Bathed in amber light, they glowed with a warmth that rivaled the candle table toppers. Even if the rest of the patrons weren't dressed in business attire, Abby would be underdressed. The setting was much too intimate and lush. Quickly, she checked the front of her uniform to make sure it was at least clean, then buttoned her cardigan tight.

A short ball of a man in a black suit greeted them with a smile. "Good evening, Mr. Smith. You picking up to go?"

"Not tonight, Vishay. We're going to eat here."

With a deferring nod, the man led them to a table near the back of the restaurant, next to a bronze statue of what Abby assumed was some kind of Indian god or goddess. It didn't escape her notice that Hunter, though as underdressed as she was, looked perfectly at home. Worse, he looked better than all the other men in the room. Any glances in his direction were admiring ones, and there'd been quite a few.

"First-name basis," Abby noted after Vishay departed. "You come here a lot?"

"Two, three nights a week when I'm in the city."

And breakfast every morning at Guy's. "Not much for home cooking, are you?"

"Never really had the chance to learn. Eating out is easier."

For him maybe; certainly not his wallet. Abby's eyes bugged when she saw the prices on the menu.

"Is something wrong? Don't you like Indian food?" Hunter asked.

"Wouldn't know. I've never eaten Indian food." What she did know was that Hunter had very expensive tastes when it came to take-out restaurants.

"Warren wasn't big on eating out," she explained when Hunter looked surprised. "Said he did enough of that at work and didn't see the need. Not when I could cook for him." She unfolded an amethyst napkin and covered her lap. "I used to think that was a compliment until I realized he simply didn't want to spend the money.

"On me, anyway," she added, smoothing the purple wrinkles.

She felt Hunter studying her again. "What?" she asked, looking up. He wore a perplexed expression, one that made his eyes gray and unreadable. "Did I say something wrong?"

"I'm trying to figure out how someone like you got stuck spending six years with that idiot."

"I told you. He didn't start out a bully. He grew into the role over time."

"Still, you don't seem the type to be bullied."

Oh, how little he knew. "Guess I grew into the role, too." That's what happened when you believed you couldn't do better. "Warren was the only person I knew in the city."

"You didn't have friends?"

"No one close. There were a few women in the building, but no one I felt comfortable going to."

"What about your parents?"

She didn't mean for her laugh to come out so sharply, but it did nonetheless. "Let's say my mother and I have similar taste in men and leave it at that."

She saw him digesting the information. "So you stayed because you didn't have anywhere to go."

"Partly." If it was only that simple, she thought, playing with the edge of her napkin. "Warren was the first man who… He

had me convinced I couldn't do any better."
A weight settled on her shoulders.

"Hey." To her surprise, Hunter reached
across the table and covered her hand.
"You've already done better."

"I have?"

"Sure." His expression was deadly serious.
"You dumped his sorry behind, didn't you?"

She was struck by how much the candlelight made his eyes sparkle. An optical illu-
sion, no doubt, but mesmerizing all the same.
She found herself falling into them. "Thank
you."

He pulled his hand away, leaving her skin
cool once more.

Scrambling for some sort of mental pur-
chase, she changed the subject. "How about
we talk about something else instead?"

"Like what?"

"How about you?" she asked.

Hunter lay down the menu. "Not much to
talk about."

"There's got to be something." An entire
day together and she knew very little about
the man. He spoke little, revealed less.

Case in point, the way he shrugged off her
request. "Not really."

"How long you been taking photographs?"

"My whole life. My father bought me my

first 35 millimeter when I was eight. I blew a whole roll taking pictures of my mother's Pomeranian. Dad told me later I should have used better lighting."

"He was a photographer, too?"

"You ever see the photo of the schoolkids saluting the president?"

"Sure. It's famous." Her eyes widened again. "He took that?"

"Among others."

"Wow. I'm impressed."

"Yeah. It's a memorable shot." For a moment, he seemed to lose himself in the candle flame. "Anyway, I got started by studying him. I used to travel as part of his crew when I was on school break."

She noticed Hunter said *part of his crew,* not *with him.* Abby wondered if there was a story behind his choice of words. If she knew him better, she'd ask. "And what do you take pictures of?" she asked instead. "Besides unsuspecting waitresses."

"Anything and everything. Wherever the job sends me."

A waiter suddenly appeared. He wore a bright gold jacket and carried a bread basket that matched. Everything in the place seemed to glisten in jewel tones. Between the surroundings and the man across from her, she felt like a unkempt, drab mop. If the food was gorgeous-looking, too, she was out of there.

It didn't help that the host had placed them in what she swore was the most intimate corner of the restaurant. She and Hunter sat tucked behind a potted plant, in a nook illuminated by jeweled votive candles. Hunter's eyes changed color in the soft light, turning indigo to match their surroundings. She tried to shift her position, but her foot brushed his, making her doubly aware of the closed space.

The waiter placed the basket in front of her. "Naan," he explained.

Abby unfolded the napkin to reveal an aroma that made her mouth water. "Indian bread," Hunter told her. "Best I've had outside of New Delhi."

"You've been to India?" She wasn't surprised. Seeing how at ease he appeared in these surroundings, she could easily imagine him in exotic lands. *A real-life action hero.*

"Couple times on assignment," he said, tearing off a chunk of flat bread and handing it to her. "Once to northern India and once to New Delhi. Beautiful country."

He was right. The bread was delicious. She reached for another piece. "Must be nice. Traveling all over the world. Photographing exotic places."

"I'm not sure you'd call my last few assignments exotic. I've been doing a lot of work for *Newstime*. In fact, I leave in a few days for a swing through the Middle East."

"Sounds pretty exotic to me."

"Sure, if you like dodging potential violence."

"Yeah, I wouldn't know anything about that," she drawled.

Hunter cocked his head, eyes catching the candle flame. The shift brought out the blue even more. "Are you always this sarcastic?"

"Unfortunately." Warren called it her smart mouth. "I try to bite my tongue, but for some reason, with you the tone slips out."

"Should I be flattered or insulted?"

"I'll let you decide," she told him. Mainly because she didn't know the answer herself. She didn't know why she was so free with her thoughts today. Fatigue? Not having to fear a reprisal? With Warren she was always so careful about her words, never knowing when she'd say something to set him off. She was pretty certain all Hunter would do was snark back.

Or maybe it was the fact she didn't feel the need to impress. Rather, knowing she had no need to impress, she didn't have to worry about trying.

Perhaps she should try. A little. The man had spent the day at the courthouse with her. Then again, the day at the courthouse was largely his fault. Besides, he wasn't exactly putting his best foot forward for her, either. And after tonight, they'd probably never see each other again. He'd be off living his exotic adventurous life, and she'd be at McKenzie House, sitting in the common room circling Help Wanted ads. The agreeable mood she'd been nursing faded away.

Dinner was delicious, as always, although Hunter's companion didn't seem to enjoy the food as much as he hoped she would. Abby retreated into herself and never completely returned, and he...well, he apparently was battling his conscience. Why his chest knotted up every time Abby's face sobered, he couldn't explain. After all, it wasn't his fault Guy was a self-serving slug. Hunter hadn't asked the diner owner to fire Abby, any more than he'd asked her d-bag of an ex-boyfriend to track her down. She—they—were not Hunter's problem. So why did every crestfallen expression that crossed her features have him feeling like Attila the Hun? Worse, why did he feel the insane need to take her out to dinner? Here, where the candlelight turned her hair the color of warm caramel?

That reminded him: he needed to have a talk with Vishay. The man had sat them at the smallest, most candlelit table in the restaurant. Beneath the table, their knees touched. Above, every little movement caused their personal spaces to collide. Hunter spent the meal far more aware of her body than he should be. Every brush of her leg against his jeans reminded him of how it had felt when he was holding her earlier. He'd reacted with a lot more than compassion. At least his body had. How could he not? With her head tucked beneath his chin as if she was a perfect fit. Her hair…damn, the way her curls tickled his skin. Like baby-soft strands of silk. The mere memory made his fingers twitch. What he wouldn't give to smooth his hands through the untamed strands to learn for himself if the softness lived up to its potential.

How long had it been since he'd touched a woman, anyway? Five, six months? Longer.

Too long, apparently. Unfortunately, he wasn't kidding about the baggage. Abby had a freaking wardrobeful. He wasn't into taking on other people's burdens. It was enough shouldering his own.

Nope. If he wanted to scratch his itch, he

would have to find somewhere else. Wasn't like he didn't have plenty of opportunity. There were always women—available women—drawn by either the excitement of his profession or his money, who were more than willing to visit his bed for a night or two.

"It's after seven," he said, looking at his watch. "Think the sheriff's paid your ex a visit?"

"Hope so. They didn't give a time." She poked at a piece of chicken with her fork. "Warren's going to be furious," she said in a low voice.

"Who cares how Warren feels? His feelings aren't your problem anymore."

"Old habits are hard to break. You're right, though. Warren brought his problems on himself. I've got far bigger ones to worry about."

The twisting sensation seized his chest again. "I can talk to Guy. Smooth things over. Explain."

"You'd do that?"

"I offered, didn't I?" No need to tell her he was as surprised by his offer as she was.

Abby shook her head. "Thanks, but I doubt he'll listen to you any more than he listened to me. Looks like I'll have to start from scratch. By the way, since I can't list Guy, I'm putting you down as a reference."

"Me? What am I supposed to say?"

"I don't know. Tell people what a great waitress you thought I was. How I'm efficient and invaluable."

"You kept forgetting people's orders."

"Only at the beginning," she replied, eyes narrowing. "And you owe me."

Hunter decided not to argue the point. "Fine. If a prospective employer tracks me down while I'm in Tripoli, I'll tell them you were the best waitress I ever had. How's that?"

"No need to exaggerate. Just be realistic." She leaned back in her seat, looking as if she was about to withdraw again. "I doubt you'll get many calls, anyway. The job market for unskilled help is pretty competitive."

"I doubt you're that unskilled," he said. He didn't like that her expression was getting to him again.

"Weren't you listening? Guy's was the first job I ever held. Taking care of Warren doesn't count. Unless you know someone who needs a glorified housekeeper, chief cook and bottle washer."

"Actually…" Hunter sat back without finishing his statement. He wasn't sure if she was hinting or if his mind came up with the thought on its own. Either way, he thought as he studied her candlelit face, the idea was a bad one. A truly bad idea.

On the other hand—he considered the disorganization taking over his loft—Christina did say he needed a housekeeper more than an assistant. It would be a temporary fix at most, a win-win for them both while she looked for a real job.

Besides, he was leaving the country. By the time he got back, he'd have scratched his itch and put an end to the twisting, unsettled feeling that gripped him every time he looked in Abby's direction. And she couldn't say he hadn't made amends for Guy firing her.

From across the table, her big brown eyes watched him with interest. Waiting on what he'd started to say.

"Actually…" Leaning forward, he started again. "I have a proposition for you."

CHAPTER FOUR

"YOU'RE EARLY."

Abby flashed a nervous grin. When Hunter suggested she work for him—temporarily—she'd accepted immediately. What could she say? Recent unemployment and the threat of poverty made her overeager. This morning, however, she wondered if she should have thought things through a little better.

Especially since her new employer answered the door half-dressed.

To be fair, she *was* early, although no more than twenty minutes or so. Again, she blamed unemployed eagerness.

"Just trying to impress the boss," she said.

Amazingly, she managed to answer without stuttering. Based on his damp hair, Hunter had been in the shower when she rang the front doorbell. Droplets of water clung to the brown hair dusting his chest, and she was pretty sure she saw one drip traveling downward, toward what she was sure was a very contoured abdomen. Visions of last night's embrace popped into her head. She'd leaned against that torso. Spread her palms across those shoulders.

"You could have told me to wait outside," she told him.

"Next time I will. Is that coffee for me?" He gestured to the cardboard tray in her hand.

"Yes." Abby felt her cheeks grow warm, although that could be from the near nakedness as much as anything. "I was getting myself some, and figured you'd be looking for breakfast. Since Guy threw you out, too."

"My money would have put me back in Guy's good graces quickly enough."

True, but she needed breakfast and she wasn't in Guy's good graces. "Does that mean you don't want your fried egg sandwich?"

"You got me a sandwich?"

"With cheese on whole wheat. Not exactly your usual order, but it was the best I could do while commuting."

"That's…" There was an unreadable expression in his eyes as he looked in the bag. "Thank you," he said, turning those eyes back to hers. "That's very nice of you."

You'd think no one had ever been nice to him before. Or that she'd ever received a compliment, for that matter, seeing how her blush shot straight to her toes. Come to think of it, she couldn't remember the last time she *had* received a compliment.

"I thought you were broke."

She gave her best shrug. "I found temporary employment. And, like I said, I'm simply trying to get on the boss's good side."

"Food isn't necessary. Just do your job and clean my apartment."

Did he have any idea how liberating such a simple request sounded? To simply do anything without worrying about reprisal was all she ever wanted. "You got a deal," she said, smiling. Her eyes locked with his. Their color was definitely bluer today than last night. Bluer and darker.

The heat of the air in the hallway kicked up a notch.

"You, um…" Maybe it was the woodsy smell of his aftershave mingling with breakfast, but she suddenly remembered Hunter's state of dress. "Could you…?"

"Right." He blinked, as if realizing himself, and backed away. "Of course. Come inside while I put a shirt on."

Don't rush on my account, Abby almost said. Fortunately, she didn't.

While Hunter jogged upstairs, she wandered into the kitchen area, looking for a place to set the coffee down. She needed a good dose of caffeine to clear the topless-Hunter images from her head. Today was supposed to be fresh start number two. No way she was ruining the milestone by acting like a flustered schoolgirl. The squirrelly sensations in her stomach would simply have to go away.

She wasn't stupid. She knew exactly what was happening to her. Her libido, after years of being bullied into dormancy, had decided to wake up. Hardly surprising, when she thought about it. A woman would have to be literally dead not to feel some kind of physical awareness around a man who looked like Hunter. It was like being attracted to a movie star or a handsome model in a magazine advertisement. Enjoyable but unrealistic.

What shocked her, though, was the intensity with which she reacted. She didn't simply look at him with attraction; she felt it all the way to her bones. Her skin grew hot every time he glanced at her, and her insides seemed on a perpetual trampoline. She hadn't felt this much with Warren ever. Thank goodness Hunter was leaving town in a couple days. Her attraction was obviously making up for lost time by overreacting.

On the plus side, she could, with relief, say

that her years with Warren hadn't deadened her completely. That was one piece of baggage she could unpack.

In the meantime, she needed to act professionally. She was here to clean and organize, not fantasize. Setting her packages on the black marble countertop, she looked around her temporary assignment. Hunter's apartment was not what she expected. In her imagination, she'd pictured him living in some rugged man-cave, a location that matched his action star exterior. She certainly didn't expect an airy, light-filled loft. It had one of those open floor plans where one large space was meant to be broken up by furniture into smaller living areas. Hunter hadn't broken up anything, however. He barely had furniture.

It was pretty obvious why he needed a housekeeper, though, because what he did have was clutter. A lot of clutter. There were piles stacked all over the place. In one corner sat a workstation piled high with miscellaneous items, half of which she didn't recognize but assumed were photo related. Probably equipment that spilled over from the collection of cameras and materials on the shelf above.

It was as though he'd decided to decorate with clutter instead of real furnishings.

And yet, in spite of the mess, the apartment felt empty. Incomplete. As if it was missing something besides furniture.

She was in the kitchen studying the impressive array of unused appliances when Hunter reappeared. He'd slipped into a faded T-shirt. The tight red cotton still obscenely emphasized his body, but at least he was dressed. "Getting the lay of the land?"

"I'm trying. This kitchen is a cook's dream."

"So the Realtor told me." He was busy digging into the sack for his egg sandwich.

"I take it that wasn't a big selling point for you." Wonder what was? Meanwhile, watching him devour his poorly prepared breakfast, she got an idea. "If you'd like, I could cook for you. I mean," she added when he looked up, "while you're in town. For a change of pace."

"I didn't hire you to cook."

"I know. I'm not a gourmet cook, either. But you've got to admit, a home-cooked meal before leaving for the desert might be nice, don't you think? Comfort food for the road?"

"I wouldn't know. I've never had a home-cooked meal."

"You're joking." He was, right? The look on his face said no. "Never?"

"Not really. They don't have personal chefs at boarding school."

"You went to boarding school?" How sad.

"When I wasn't on the road with my father. You needn't look so horrified," Hunter added. "They're not all Dickensian nightmares."

Abby wasn't quite sure what he meant by his comment, but she did know he wasn't as indifferent about the experience as he'd like to appear. The way he fiddled with his sandwich wrapper gave him away. Hard to picture the strong, aloof man she'd spent yesterday with being affected by anything. But then, as she'd already noted, she didn't know him, did she?

The apartment's incompleteness hit her again.

"How about I cook you your first one today?" she said, returning to the topic at hand. "Nothing fancy. Spaghetti and meatballs? A side salad. It's a shame to waste all these fancy appliances."

"Not to mention it would add another item to your job description for when I write you a reference."

Cheeks warming, she found it was her turn to study the counter. "I did call myself a chief cook and bottle washer. Kind of implies cooking."

"Suppose it does." Hunter gave a sigh, but his expression was one of amusement. The crooked smile brightened his face. If possible the look was even sexier than his bare torso. The squirrelly sensation returned, causing her knees to buckle a little. Dear Lord, but he was too gorgeous for words.

"So it's a deal?" she asked, clearing her throat.

"Sure," Hunter replied. "Spaghetti and meatballs it is."

"Great. I'll cook for you tonight."

As if on cue, the squirrels began dashing around even faster.

"I think I'm signing you up for that reality show about hoarders," Abby remarked an hour later.

Hunter didn't even look up from the spreadsheet he was working on. "You're exaggerating."

"Barely." All right, she was exaggerating, but seriously, did the man not know the meaning of the term *file cabinet?* Before she could do any kind of serious cleaning, she realized, she had to take care of the piles. What she'd discovered was that Hunter's apartment wasn't so much messy as it was simply chaotic. Needless to say, most of the equipment was job related. There were research books, photo proofs, magazine articles. Then there was the equipment, and equipment-related stuff—the unrecognizable junk on his work-station table. Who knew there were so many different kinds of camera lenses? And lens films. What the heck? Wasn't film for inside the camera?

"Did you know," she continued, picking up another travel magazine, "they invented this new machine a few years ago. Called a paper shredder."

"Very amusing. I told you. I'm only here between assignments. The apartment's nothing more than a place to stow my stuff."

"Pretty expensive storage space. Wouldn't one of those rental units work better?"

"The building's an investment." He looked up from the screen. "You never talked this much when you were a waitress."

Meaning she was talking too much now. Abby felt her cheeks grow hot. "Sorry," she murmured. Biting her lip, she went back to her cleaning.

Behind her, Hunter let out a breath. "You don't need to apologize," he said.

"Sorry. Force of habit."

"Let me guess. Warren didn't like you talking, either."

"Said he needed quiet after a hard day at work." Thinking of all the aspects of her life her ex-boyfriend had controlled, Abby cringed. Thank God he was out of her life for good.

"Hey." Hunter's voice, soft and low, sounded behind her. "You don't have to stop talking."

"But you said…"

He touched her shoulder. "I'm not Warren."

No, he definitely wasn't. Far from it. For starters, Warren's touch was never as gentle, nor had it sent warmth spiraling around her spine.

"I—I found a bunch of receipts," she said, edging away before she grew too used to the feeling. "Underneath a pile of photos. Are they important?"

"Probably. What are the photos of?"

"A demonstration."

"Right. Damascus, last month. I should submit those."

He said it casually. Abby handed him the paperwork, glancing again at the photos. The images were violent and rueful. It was jarring to think a person could be having breakfast at a streetside café one moment and photographing brutality the next.

One picture showed a man being dragged away, blood staining his torn jeans. "Do you ever get worried, taking photos at events like this?"

"No."

"I would."

"I worry about missing the shot."

"Would that be so bad?"

Hunter, who'd been settling back into his seat, stopped what he was doing to stare at her in disbelief. "Yes, it would. It's my job to get the shot."

"Even if it means putting your life at risk?" No photo seemed that important.

"Doesn't matter. They aren't paying me to run away. The only thing that counts is getting the shot. And since you never know when that perfect shot is going to happen, the only thing you can do is click till you run out of memory space."

How ironic. It sounded as if the action-hero costume fit, after all. He really was literally dodging bullets. "Did you learn that lesson from your father?" She'd borrowed a computer last night and done a little research, enough to know Joseph Smith's famous photograph was only one of many famous shots he was known for. Hunter, she'd discovered, was famous, too, a little fact he never mentioned. She found site after site celebrating his coverage of a school explosion in Somalia.

"My father was right. You can't do your job if you're worried about staying safe."

"I'm sure your mother disagreed."

A curtain came down over his features. "Seeing as how she was dead at the time, I doubt it."

"Oh. Right." *Idiot.* The internet didn't mention his mother, but Abby should have put two and two together based on his comment yesterday.

Somehow, though, she imagined that had his mother lived, she would have objected. Especially seeing as Hunter's father died while on assignment. That Hunter's life might end under similar circumstances…for what? A photograph? The idea bothered Abby. Seemed sad and rather senseless, if you asked her. "The way you talk, you make it sound like your life doesn't matter," she said.

"Photography is my life," he relied.

Now that truly didn't seem right. She refrained from saying so, though. The photos, she realized, were still in her hand. As she moved to set them down, she found herself turning over the top one. The image was too harsh to look at. "I don't think I could do it," she decided.

"Do what?"

"Stand there and take pictures without being afraid. Or affected. I mean, how do

you look at what's going on around you without reacting?"

"You learn."

"How?" She wanted to know. Had his father taught him that lesson, too?

But Hunter had turned back to the computer screen. "You just do," he told her.

Once again a curtain had dropped over his
features, closing his expression to scrutiny.
There was more to his story. His answer was
too emphatic, too absolute. Had something
happened to hammer home the lesson? She
wondered if she'd ever find out.

They worked in silence for the next couple
hours. Hunter wasn't sure if Abby's silence
was in response to his comment about talking too much—he hoped not; the way she'd
shrunk back in apology made his stomach
hurt—or if she was thinking about their other
conversation. It was clear she didn't approve
of his answers, even if what he told her was
the truth. What other answer did she expect?
Might as well ask a soldier if he worried about
being shot in battle.

How many times had he watched his father risk life and limb for the perfect picture?
When Hunter was a kid, his father's risk-
taking used to scare him. But oh, the shots

he'd pulled off. *Makes all the risk worth it,* he'd overheard his dad tell a coworker once. Okay, so sometimes he did wonder if, had his mother lived, his father would be as daring. He'd certainly seemed more cautious when she was around. Ultimately, however, the answer didn't matter. His mother had died, his father had lived for his job, and Hunter understood why he'd taken the risks. Abby would understand, too, if she were a photographer. Maybe he should put a camera in her hands, train her to be one. He shook off the notion as quickly as it popped into his head. Why should he care whether she understood or not?

A flash of red caught the corner of his eye. Abby on her knees in front of his filing cabinet. She'd taken it upon herself to organize the film and stock images he'd neglected. Already proving herself a better hire than Christina.

And once she was finished, he would get a proper cleaning service. Preferably one where the employees' rear ends didn't look so enticing. Today was the first time he'd seen Abby dressed in something other than that shapeless waitress uniform. He missed the blue-and-white sack. Today's turtleneck and narrow-legged jeans revealed way too much. What he'd assumed was angular and too skinny was really long and lean. The big glimpse of leg she'd flashed in the cab? Tip of the iceberg. One thing for sure, legs like that should not be encased in attention-getting red. He must have made a dozen inputting errors because the color distracted him.

"Hunter?"

Breaking off from his thoughts, he turned his attention to the file cabinet. With a photo clutched in her hand, Abby was staring at him as if he had two heads. Dammit. How long had she been talking?

"Should I label the back of the photos with yellow notes like the ones already in the file?" she asked.

Thank goodness it was a question where he didn't have to be listening in order to answer. "For now. The notes are reminders for labels." Another project Christina had failed to complete. With luck, karma had gifted his old assistant with an equally distracted and inept assistant of her own.

"Looks like I have another project to tackle while you're gone," Abby said, grabbing a pen and yellow notepad.

"Unless you find a job before then."

"I meant if I didn't find a permanent position." Her expression faltered again. Hunter wished she'd stop looking so forlorn. Made his gut hurt.

Why had he said anything in the first place? They both knew the job was temporary. He didn't need to remind her.

Maybe you were reminding yourself? As his gaze dropped to the brass grommets dotting her back pockets, he wondered if the reminder wasn't to keep him from doing something stupid.

"Where was this picture taken?"

Abby held up the photo in her hand.

"Let me see." Joining her, he took it from her and saw it was a black-and-white shot of an old man enjoying a cigarette while sitting on a stack of luggage.

He smiled, remembering. "Mirpur Khas," he said. "Waiting on the rail platform. We got to the station before sunrise and he was sitting there, patient as can be. When the sun got bright enough, I snapped his picture. He didn't even blink."

Reaching around her shoulder, Hunter pointed to the band on the man's wrist. "See? You can read the time on his watch? And how wizened his skin is? I remember seeing those wrinkles and thinking he looked like he'd been waiting forever."

"Maybe he had," Abby replied. She turned

to Hunter, and he found himself nearly nose to nose. "Do you remember every picture you take?"

"The memorable ones stick in your head." *Like yours,* he thought. Looking at her now, he saw glimpses of the same wistfulness and steel. She still wasn't wearing much makeup. He liked that. Showed the imperfections and emphasized the character of her face. No wizened skin here. What would if feel like if he traced the back of his hand across her cheek? Would her skin feel as soft as he imagined?

To his disappointment, she turned away, back to the photographs.

"Now that one," he said, recognizing the shot of elephants marching in the mist, "was taken in the Congo rain forest. I waited two days in the rain for those blasted creatures. Caught a wicked case of paddy foot from standing in the mud and had to spend the next week changing my socks twice a day."

"Better paddy foot than getting shot."

Back to that, was she? "Better I came away with the photo," he reminded her. "I could have sat in the rain for nothing, which happens more than you know. A lot of this job is plain old luck. Being in the right place at the right time."

"And yet you stick with it. Guess the job can't be all bad."

Hunter slipped the photo from her fingers. "It has its moments, that's for certain." Good and bad.

He waited as she wrote "Africa: Wildlife" on a sticky note, then handed her back the picture.

"I'm curious," she said. "Under what category would you file my photo?"

"Why do you want to know?"

"Well, as far as filing goes, you've got old men, old women, street people, occupations."

"Standard stock categories."

"I was wondering what category you'd stick me in. Women at work, street scenes or—" she scanned the tabs "—New Yorkers."

"None of the above. You'd get your own special category."

"I would?" She blushed, making him wish he had a camera then and there instead of across the room. The soft pink suited her. People should compliment her more often, to draw out the shade.

"Uh-huh. I'd file you under strangely compelling waitresses."

Another blush, followed by a swipe of her bangs and a duck of her face. A trifecta of shyness. So sexy he felt his jeans tighten.

"You mean the photo, right?" she said in a low voice.

Catching her chin with his finger, he lifted her face back to his. "Sure." In reality, he found far more than the photo compelling. But saying so would only open a dangerous can of worms.

Perhaps she realized it as well, because her smile was tinged with gratitude. "I'll make sure to label it appropriately should I run across a copy."

"Actually, you'll find a few copies on the printer. From the other day when I was working."

The look she gave him, as she scampered over to check, said *really?* "I lost my copy during the fight."

"You can take one of those if you'd like," he told her. "Personally, I think the black-and-white version has more depth. Highlights the contrasts."

"You mean the bags under my eyes."

This dumping on her appearance was becoming a habit. "Are you always so negative about the way you look?"

"Generally. Another force of habit, I'm afraid. Along with jumping when called and blaming myself for mistakes.

"I'm working on it, though," she added over her shoulder.

"As for the photographs…" She left the page in the tray. "Thanks, but I'll pass. Not sure it's a memory I want to keep, if you know what I mean."

He did indeed. Photography had the power to instantly transport you to a place or time, even ones you wished you could forget. "I'll take another of you if you want," he offered. "One with a nicer memory."

"No sense pressing your luck. I can't guarantee I'll take a second good shot."

There she went, denigrating herself again. Warren and whoever else had put those thoughts in her head should be shot.

Moving back to his computer chair, Hunter told her, "I can."

"How confident of you," she said with a laugh.

"Simply stating a fact."

"Of course you are. I think I'll go back to filing."

"Suit yourself." He'd take a shot of her sometime when she wasn't paying attention. He preferred candid, unaffected ones, anyway.

He returned to his expense reports. Had

to admit, the numbers weren't nearly as interesting.

"Uh-oh," Abby said a few minutes later. "One of your files is missing a tab."

"Must have fallen off."

"Either that or your former assistant never created one. Did you know she couldn't spell?"

"Doesn't—"

"Wow!" Abby's gasp of amazement cut him off. "These photos are…"

He wondered what he'd photographed that she found so impressive. "Are what?"

"The kids playing soccer. They look so happy."

Kids? Hunter's insides turned icy. Couldn't be. He'd ordered those photos thrown away.

Even as he dreaded seeing the images, some perverse need made him get up to look. Over Abby's shoulder he saw what she didn't. The hard black eyes hadn't changed a bit. Hatred hidden behind a broad smile. The memory came flooding back. *Mr. Hunter! Mr. Hunter!*

"Throw them out," he said.

"Why? They look perfectly good to me."

"I said throw them out!"

Abby sat back on her heels, eyes wide in confusion. Hunter immediately felt like a jerk.

Wasn't her fault. She didn't know. "Sorry," he said, washing his hand over his features.

"Is something wrong? I don't understand."

"Nothing's wrong. Just— I don't want to keep the photos, okay?"

The walls started closing in. He needed fresh air. A break. "I'm going to go out for a bit," he told her. "Lock the door behind you when you leave for the day."

Grabbing the one anchor he could always count on, his camera, he headed for the door. As he closed it behind him, the last thing he saw was Abby, still kneeling on the floor, surrounded by photos and questions.

CHAPTER FIVE

ABBY MADE SPAGHETTI and meatballs, anyway. She'd promised, and she intended to keep her word. If Hunter returned in time for dinner, terrific. If not, at least his gourmet kitchen got one good use. Besides, it wouldn't be the first time she'd spent time and energy on a meal that was ignored.

Although in this case, the circumstances were a bit different. Hunter wasn't ignoring her, nor did he storm out in anger. On the contrary, he'd been upset for a different reason. The minute he saw those photographs, his entire demeanor had changed. He went from warm and open to closed off in the blink of an eye. Why? What about those pictures set him off?

Hunter had told her to throw the photos away, but curiosity wouldn't let her. Once she'd finished making the sauce, she turned to study the pictures across the countertop, looking for something that might explain Hunter's agitation. The shots were of kids playing soccer in what looked like Africa. What could possibly be so upsetting about kids playing a game?

She thought about the moments just before she'd found the file. It'd been a pleasure to work around him. While he spoke little, his presence was comfortable, friendly. Then, when he knelt behind her on the floor... She used to hate it when Warren approached her from behind. Mainly because if she couldn't see his face, she couldn't judge his mood. A hand gripping her shoulder could mean anger as easily as it meant anything else. But when Hunter knelt behind her, she didn't so much as tense. At least not with uncertainty. Instead, it brought her back to this morning in his doorway, when he'd greeted her damp and half-naked. Even now, in a kitchen smelling of tomatoes and garlic, she could, if she concentrated, recall his aftershave. How the scent had teased her nostrils when he reached around her to point out landmarks. Much like the way his breath had tickled her temple when he spoke.

Focus, Abby. Bad enough her libido caused problems when Hunter was in the room; she didn't need it flaring to life while thinking of the man, too.

She returned to the photos. There was a woman in several of the shots. Tall and voluptuous, she had auburn hair and a toothy grin that leaped off the page. Was she the bad memory? A broken heart would certainly explain his distant nature.

What kind of woman would Hunter fall for? Abby traced the image. That she'd be beautiful was a given. This woman's looks, however, went beyond surface pretty. One glance at her photos told you she had a special sort of vitality. Her eyes literally sparkled with life. A far cry from Abby's dead insides, that's for sure.

Keys sounded in the lock, causing her to drop the photo she was holding and jump back. Hunter walked in, camera around his neck. He looked tired, as if he'd walked a marathon. One he'd lost. Abby wasn't used to seeing his shoulders slumped with such weariness. She grabbed the counter edge to keep from wrapping him in a hug.

"Hey," she murmured softly.

"You're still here."

Not the most enthusiastic of greetings. "Promised you dinner, remember?"

"So I can smell. You didn't have to go the trouble."

"We're talking spaghetti sauce, not a gourmet meal. Besides, I enjoyed being able to cook again." McKenzie House didn't have much of a setup beyond the basics. Anything that involved more than a microwave and a jar was a treat to make, as far as she was concerned. "Hopefully, you'll like how everything turned out, because I made a lot. And by a lot, I mean a lot. You'll be eating leftovers for a week." She was babbling, trying to fill the awkwardness with noise. The fact that Hunter hadn't moved since setting his camera down didn't help. He simply stood in the kitchen entrance, staring.

Shoot. Abby followed his gaze, and realized he'd spied the photographs. Quickly she moved to gather them. "Sorry, I didn't get to throw those away yet. Let me do it right now."

Hunter reached over and stopped her. "S'all right. I'll take care of them." Except he didn't, continuing instead to stare off into space. Abby wished she knew what he was thinking. He felt so far away.

"I shouldn't have walked out the way I did," he said after a few minutes.

"No big deal. You didn't swear or throw

anything. Makes it a step up from most of my walkouts."

He arched a brow. The gesture almost—almost—breached the distance he'd retreated behind. "Just because I wasn't violent doesn't make it right. You shouldn't roll over so easily."

"You think I'm rolling over?"

"I was rude, and you made me spaghetti. What would you call it?"

What she'd call it was deflecting the focus away from himself. She "rolled over" and left the challenge unspoken. "Next time I'll skip the cooking. Would that be better?"

Hunter didn't answer, his attention having returned to the images spread across the counter. Coming around to join him on his side, Abby picked up the shot that seemed to be holding his attention. It was a close-up of the woman, with several young children gathered around her. A wave of envy washed over Abby as she was yet again struck by the woman's vitality.

"She's very beautiful," she said.

"Her name was Donna."

Was. No mistaking the finality in his voice. Abby turned the photo over, ashamed that she'd been envious of a dead woman.

"I shouldn't have said anything." No matter how curious she was, she had no business picking the scab of an old wound. Better to let him process the past in peace. "I'll go check on the sauce."

"I took these shots in Somalia," Hunter said, stopping her.

Somalia. Hearing the name gave her a déjà vu feeling. Nonetheless, Abby shook her head and told him, "You don't need to explain." Knowing what dragging up the past was like, she felt the need to let him off the hook.

"On the contrary, I think I should explain more. I *want* to explain more."

"Why?" No one had ever bothered explaining their behavior to her before. She leaned a hip against the countertop. "Is this because I shared my sad story with you? Because if that's your reason, there's no need to go tit for tat."

"I know, and you're rolling over again."

"No, I'm offering you an out."

He half smiled. "So you are. Thank you."

Abby felt a warmth settle over her. It was nice to have her consideration acknowledged, despite the sober circumstances. "You're welcome. And I'm sorry if the photos brought back bad memories."

"They did." She waited while he set the overturned photograph right side up again. "It was my first assignment after my father's accident. I thought I was prepared. I'd seen war and horrible conditions before, so I figured I knew what I was getting into. The people, though..." He blew out a long breath through his nose. "When I traveled with my father, the attention was on his work. Even if I was taking my own shots, it was second to what he needed to do. That's how being an assistant worked. Something Christina, my old assistant, never understood.

"Anyway, for the first time in my life I was the lead photographer. The one who did the talking, the interacting. I was supposed to spend a couple weeks there, but I stretched it out."

"Sounds like the place made an impact on you."

"Not the place, the people," he replied. "They were so grateful, so eager to learn. The kids, especially. Like little sponges, absorbing everything. Slightest little thing would make their faces light up. Could be anything. A piece of chocolate, a book, even something like a soccer game."

"And Donna?" Had she made as powerful an impact? He'd yet to say, and Abby was surprised at how anxious she was to find out.

"Donna taught at the school. Second or

third grade, I can't remember which. Maybe both. Didn't matter. The entire school loved her. Camera loved her, too, in case you didn't notice."

"So that's why there are so many photos of her?"

"Did you think...?" He shook his head. "No, she wasn't. Not the way you think. Yes, she and I—"

"I get the picture." They'd been lovers; she wasn't the love of his life.

"Given my reaction, I could see why you might think otherwise."

"Why did you react so badly?" So far, he'd revealed nothing but a fondness for the school and the country. Sliding onto a nearby stool, Abby eagerly waited for more.

"Like I said, the place was special. I didn't expect to get so sucked in, but there was something addictive about the sense of community. It was like being in the middle of this giant family."

Which, to a man who'd recently lost his father, must have been incredibly appealing. Abby could relate. Loneliness was an incredibly powerful weakness. Hadn't she grabbed hold of the first person she'd found to fill the emptiness in her life?

"There was this kid named Naxar," Hunter

said. "Not so much a kid, actually. He was only a couple years younger than me. Worked as a janitor at the school. Always following me around, calling 'Mr. Hunter, Mr. Hunter!' I made him my pet project. He'd carry my equipment, help me set up."

"Your first assistant," Abby noted with a smile.

"The beginning of a very bad trend," Hunter said, giving another half smile. Like before, it failed to reach his eyes. "You'd think I'd learn."

The smile faded. "He blew himself up during a school assembly."

Dear God. Abby's stomach dropped. The explosion. The photos that had made Hunter's career.

"The evidence was there all along, but I was too involved to see it. Too busy focusing on the kids' smiles."

Hunter fished a photo out of the pile and slid it toward her. A crowd watching two boys racing after the soccer ball. Abby knew right away which young man was Naxar. While all the others were cheering, he stood on the edge of the action. Hunter's camera had caught him unaware, capturing a face icy with rage. It was that expression that had caught her attention when she first unearthed the pictures.

Looking again, this time knowing the whole story, Abby shivered. To think one man could cause such death and destruction. Even Warren, for all his rages, wasn't capable of that level of violence.

And Hunter, seeing the community he cared about blown apart... She couldn't imagine how that felt.

Or the guilt he might be feeling.

"It's not your fault," she said. Wasn't that what the abuse counselors had told her? That the victim isn't responsible for the abuser's rage? "There's no way you could have known what he planned to do."

"Not my fault, but a mistake all the same."

"What was?" She figured he would say missing the signs.

"Letting him get close. Letting any of them get close."

"You mean the people at the school?"

He nodded. "There's a reason the camera stays between you and the subject. It's your buffer. Keeps you focused on the job. I forgot."

"You make it sound like caring was a mistake."

"It was. The only thing I should have cared about was getting the shot. Everything else..."

He shrugged the rest of the thought away,

but Abby got the point. He was saying nothing else mattered but the shot, same as he'd
said before. Not his subject, not the people
around him, not his own safety. With one
raise of his shoulders, Abby suddenly understood why he wanted the photographs destroyed. He wasn't trying to bury the memory
of a woman, or even his guilt. He was burying his feelings. How well she understood
that desire. She, too, had wrapped her heart
in a blanket of numbness, stuffed it in a hole
of self-preservation, where pain couldn't find
it. Life was simpler that way.

Only for some reason, when it came to
Hunter, the desire felt wrong. Why, she
couldn't say. In fact, she couldn't say anything at all. She settled for touching his shoulder.

Hunter covered her hand with his. The cool
touch of his fingers wrapped around hers ran
straight up her arm, reminding her that while
her heart was numb, the rest of her was still
alive.

"You're not wearing a bandage today," he
said.

Changing the topic. "Didn't see the sense,"
she told him. "You know the bruises are there.
Why bother hiding them?"

Turning her hand palm up, he gave a small nod. "Your skin shouldn't have bruises."

"He says, stating the obvious." She was being flip, but inside, she'd grown warm. Could he feel her pulse beneath his fingers? If so, he would know it was racing. Shouldn't be. He was simply making an observation. There was no compliment, no seductive overtone. Her body was reacting to the tenderness.

Maybe she was the one, then, who needed distance. Especially now, as Hunter ran his thumb across the pulse point. "You deserve good things, Abby Gray. Good things. Good people. A good life. You know that, right?"

Of course she knew that. This sudden switch in conversation didn't make sense. It was almost as though he was trying to tell her something else.

"So do you," she told him.

"Don't worry about me. I get exactly what I need." Dropping her hand, he gathered up the photographs. "I'm going to get rid of these before dinner."

A few minutes later, Abby heard the high-pitched squeal of a shredder—the very machine she teased him earlier about not owning. She listened, unconsciously stroking her wrist. Got what he needed, huh? She couldn't help wondering if that was enough.

* * *

"Explain to me again why, if you hired me to be your housekeeper, we're taking a walk in Central Park?" Abby stood on the top of the apartment building's steps, watching Hunter fiddle with his camera.

"I told you," he replied, "I get stir-crazy if I stay inside too long."

"I got the stir-crazy part. What I don't get is why I needed to come along. Shouldn't I be, I don't know, cleaning your house?" Which she'd been doing, until he'd insisted she join him.

"You have a problem with taking a break?"

"Suppose not."

He watched a squirrel drag a piece of pizza crust across the sidewalk.

"Are you planning a long walk?" They seemed to be walking at a very determined pace for just a simple stroll.

"Does it matter?"

"It does if you want me to get dinner started for you."

Hunter stopped in his tracks. For a second, Abby thought they might turn around. "I told you yesterday, you don't have to cook for me. That's not part of the job."

"And I told you, I don't mind cooking for you."

"Well, I mind. If I'd wanted a private chef, I would have hired one." He started walking again. Abby hurried to catch up.

"Most people would enjoy the opportunity," she pointed out.

"I'm not most people."

That, she thought, looking at him from the corner of her eye, was an understatement. He was back in action-hero mode again today. Fortunately, she'd been spared a shirtless greeting when she arrived this morning. Unfortunately, he chose to wear a painted-on henley with the buttons undone. Rather than hide his muscles, the thin cotton emphasized them by rippling every time he moved. She'd decided to scrub bathrooms so she wouldn't stare.

"Besides," he added as he draped the camera strap around his neck, "it's not like you stuck around to eat."

Did he really expect her to? The mood following Hunter's story had been intimate enough. No need compounding the atmosphere by sharing dinner. It was also another reason she'd barricaded herself in the shower this morning.

His story affected her in a way she didn't expect. Until then, Hunter had been this sort of larger-than-life figure. The reluctant—

potentially tragic—knight in shining armor. Sexy but not quite real.

But then he'd told her about Naxar and she'd glimpsed a sliver of something more. Something real and familiar. She preferred sexy and illusory. She wasn't interested in feeling anything deeper than physical attraction. And so she took a page from Hunter's book and pulled back.

Until he insisted she join him for a walk. She'd caved and now was stuck strolling the park path, with him looking sexier than a man had a right to.

"I didn't realize my company was required," she replied. Or wanted, for that matter. He'd pretty much shut down himself.

The look he gave her was made unreadable by his sunglasses. "The situation reminded me too much of Reynaldo," he said.

"Who's Reynaldo?" Another assistant? He'd lost her with the reference.

"Reynaldo was the cook my mother hired the summer after fourth grade."

Abby's jaw dropped. "You had a private chef?" When he said he never had a home-cooked meal, she foolishly assumed he meant a meal not cooked at home.

"Not a chef. Reynaldo."

Sounded the same to her. "What's the difference?"

"Chefs are trained cooks. Reynaldo was..." He let out a long breath. "Reynaldo was Reynaldo."

"Meaning not trained."

"Not in the least.

And she reminded him of the man. "You're saying you don't like my cooking?"

"No, your cooking is fine."

"It's all right if you don't. Warren certainly complained enough about it." Oddly enough, Hunter's response disappointed her more.

"I said your cooking is fine. In fact, the spaghetti was delicious."

Abby couldn't help it. She smiled. "Really?"

"Yes. Trust me, your leftovers will not go to waste."

"Then I don't understand. How do I remind you of this Reynaldo?" She grabbed his arm. "Please don't say I look like him."

"Definitely not."

Again Abby smiled.

Hunter, meanwhile, had returned to fiddling with his camera settings. "My mother hired Reynaldo the year she got sick," he said in a low voice. "I ate most of my meals alone at the kitchen counter."

As he had last night.

"Oh." Abby swallowed hard. Damn, but when he dropped a comment like that into the conversation, how could she not get a lump in her throat? It was as though he was dealing out pieces of the Hunter Smith puzzle one by one. The picture she was building wasn't a cheerful one, either. "If I'd known…"

"What? You would have stayed? Kept me company?"

Abby blushed. Her answer would have been yes. He made the suggestion sound like pity, which wasn't the case. "I was going to say that I wouldn't have offered to cook in the first place," she said, scrambling to cover herself. "As far as company is concerned, I'm sure you could find some without my help."

"I'm sure I could, too."

Oh, she bet he could. She imagined he had a whole bevy of women interested in sharing a meal. Along with other things.

"Let me guess. A girl in every port, right?"

"Something like that."

Good for him, she thought, with an uncomfortable twist in her stomach. "If that's the case, then I'm off the hook, aren't I?"

"How so?"

"Well, if you were truly lonely last night,

you would have whipped out your little black book."

Pleased with herself, she skipped ahead and turned to walk backward, only to stumble over a crack in the asphalt. Her foot twisted and she fell back, arms flailing. Hunter caught her just before she landed on her backside.

Abby gasped. His arms were wrapped around her waist, pressing her tight against him. So close she could feel every contour and ridge of his muscles. His face looked down upon her. Her mouth ran dry as she imagined his silver-blue eyes looking into hers.

"What makes you think I didn't?"

Abby swallowed hard and blamed her wobbly knees on falling, not his slow growl of a response. "If you did, you certainly shipped her out early."

"Maybe I don't like overnight guests."

"Certainly would fit the profile," she retorted. "You said you kept your subjects at a distance. Why not your lovers at a distance, too?"

Hunter flashed a crooked smile as he righted her. "You might want to try walking forward. Would make the trip easier. No pun intended."

Abby blushed. Fortunately, the tumble had

knocked her hair loose from its clip, forcing her to fix the damage, and giving her an activity to hide behind. "I'll keep that in mind," she said, barrette stuck between her teeth.

At least her tumble had cooled the atmosphere. The sizzling whatever-you-want-to-call-it that rose up between their closely pressed bodies seemed to recede. If it ever existed in the first place.

For the next several yards, they walked in silence. In spite of her original reluctance, Abby had to admit the day was perfect for being outside. Overnight, Indian summer had decided to visit the city, blown in on a warm western wind. Above them, the sun hung high in a cloudless blue sky. She couldn't blame Hunter for feeling stir-crazy. It looked like half of New York had had the same idea. Central Park was full. Business people making phone calls while on park benches. Mothers pushing strollers. Couples relaxing in the sunshine. Everyone enjoying summer's last gasp.

Hunter appeared oblivious to this. Instead, far as she could tell, he appeared to be on some kind of mission. Pointing to the camera around his neck, she steered the conversation to safer topics. "You haven't snapped a single picture. Do you plan to, or do you carry it around till you see something worthy of having its picture taken?"

Again, Hunter gave her an indecipherable look. Even with his eyes mirrored, having his gaze focused so intently in her direction made her feel exposed. So much so, she almost looked away.

"Look up ahead," he told her, pointing. On the hill in front of them, a gray building rose above the tree line.

Abby felt a familiar rush. "Oh, wow, that's Belvedere Castle!"

"You know it?"

Of course she knew it. Although he didn't realize it, Hunter had guided them to one of her favorite escapes.

"I used to come here whenever things with Warren got too overwhelming." She craned her neck so she could see the main building through the trees. "Did you know the observation tower has one of the best views in the park?" When Hunter shook his head, she rolled her eyes. "Unbelievable. And you call yourself a world traveler."

Built on top of a large, craggy rock, the granite building had been part of Central Park for over a hundred years. Without giving it a second thought, Abby pulled Hunter off the path and across the grass. Leaves rustled beneath their feet as they made their way across the great lawn. "You can see practically the entire park," she told him.

Hunter could care less. He'd taken plenty of views of the park, the skyline and the castle. The only view he was interested in today involved the woman whose hand held his. She was, after all, the reason they were here. Although at the moment he was wondering if his idea was a good one.

He hadn't handled yesterday well at all. Seeing those photos from Somalia, Naxar's face, had kicked him hard. Especially since Hunter had been fighting hard all week to keep those memories from bubbling to the surface.

Interesting how they'd chosen to rise around the same time he'd met Abby. A reminder from the universe? Maybe.

Yet here he was, taking her to Belvedere Castle for a photo session. He guessed he thought the gesture might put an end to the agitation that had plagued him the past twenty hours or so. The churning, empty sensation that made him feel as if he was leaving business unfinished. In a way, he was. If she found a permanent job while he was out of the country, there was a good chance he'd never get to photograph Abby a second time, as he'd promised.

Like an artist who'd found a favorite model, he wanted another opportunity to capture her on film, in a different atmosphere, with a different emotion on her face. To see for himself if the elements would come together as seamlessly as they had before.

What he hadn't expected was for her to be so enthusiastic about the location. She practically dragged him across the grass in her rush.

Nor did he expect to be holding her hand. Her delicate fingers nestled in his felt strangely natural. Uncomfortably so. Relaxing his grip, he pulled away to regain his distance. Immediately, she blushed, then ducked his glance by brushing the hair from her face. Damn, why didn't he have his camera ready?

"I found this place totally by accident," she told him. "One day after an argument with Warren. When I saw the turret above the trees, it was like finding a little piece of magic."

"Magic?" He was surprised to hear her talk so whimsically.

"When I was a kid, I read a lot of fairy tales. Rapunzel, Sleeping Beauty, Cinderella. I wanted to believe Prince Charming existed.

That he would come riding in and whisk me off to his castle in the sky."

They reached the stone stairs. "I ended up with Warren instead. Guess we know how well that turned out, don't we?"

Hunter could tell from her frown her thoughts had gone to that dark place she went whenever Warren's name came up. How bad had things gotten? he wondered. How bad were they before that, to make running off with an overweight loser look like a better option?

Didn't matter; whatever happened was worse than she deserved, just as he'd told her last night. No woman should have bruises on her skin. And Abby had such beautifully pale skin. To think anyone would ever want to mar its surface made him want to punch Warren all over again.

"Anyway—" hearing her voice jerked him from his thoughts "—seeing a castle in the middle of New York City gave me a little hope that fairy tales might still exist for some people. Stupid, I know. Chasing Prince Charming. I'd have better luck chasing Santa Claus. Maybe I wouldn't have stuck it out with Warren as long as I did."

"Or ever come to New York," Hunter replied, not realizing until after he spoke how the comment sounded. "I mean—"

"No, you're right. A healthy dose of realism might have saved me a lot of trouble from the start."

She was right. Still, he didn't like hearing her take such a defeatist attitude. Didn't like the shadows that killed the light in her eyes.

"You wouldn't want to be a princess, anyway. Sleeping in a castle isn't all it's cracked up to be."

As though a switch had been flipped, the darkness left her expression. You had to admire her resilience, Hunter thought. She refused to be kept down.

"Please don't tell me you lived in a castle?" she said.

"For ten days. It was drafty and cold."

"When?"

"All the time."

"I meant, when did you live in a castle?"

Hunter knew exactly what she meant. He just liked how her eyes flashed when she got exasperated. "A couple of years ago. On a job. And there were no princes. Or princesses, either. Just a very cranky caretaker."

"Another fantasy bites the dust."

"Fantasies are overrated."

"Not to mention completely unrealistic,"

Abby said. "Too bad there's not always someone around to help us cope when we realize the sad truth."

Sad indeed. "Who helped you?" He had a suspicion he already knew the answer. She'd told him how isolated Warren had kept her.

"You're looking at her," Abby said with a smile.

Making his suspicion correct. He was beginning to realize the resilient woman he'd captured on film the other day was the real Abby. Took a lot of inner strength to pull yourself from a bad situation. Clearly, her strength ran even deeper than he'd thought. Made his admiration for her that much deeper, too.

They reached the terrace on the rampart. Despite being early afternoon on a weekday, the pavilion was crowded. Tourists taking pictures, mothers herding young children. A violinist had set up shop by the top of the stairs, his case open for passersby to toss in money. Hunter dug into his wallet and dropped in a few bills to say thank-you for the live soundtrack.

When he turned around, Abby was by the wall, looking out at the pond below. "Gorgeous, isn't it?"

He had to agree, though in his case, he

wasn't thinking about the landscape. He found the way Abby's skin glowed far more intriguing. She'd lit up in a way he hadn't seen before. Even her hair, which had yet again developed a mind of its own, seemed brighter. As she brushed the strands from her face, tawny highlights caught the sun.

"Drafty or not, you've got to admit having a view like this would be amazing," she said.

Amazing was the perfect word, he thought as he stood to the side and snapped away. "You'd still freeze your behind off. No window or heat."

That earned him both an eye roll and a look in his direction. "Buzzkill."

"Realist," he countered.

A second eye roll, and she returned her attention to the landscape. Hunter watched as she rose on tiptoes and leaned forward to get a better view. A move that caused her sweater to creep up her back, revealing an enticing strip of bare skin. Remembering how soft her skin felt, his body grew hard. He was beginning to see how Warren had grown so possessive. Did she have any idea how good she looked right now? Even the violinist was staring.

Hunter joined her at the wall, partly because he wanted to get closer, and partly to block the musician's view. The water below them was a smooth black mirror. Zooming in through his lens, he could make out the two of them peering over the edge. "How often did you come here?"

"More than I care to admit. Usually when Warren was at work. I'd sneak over while I was supposed to be running errands. That way if he called, I would have a reason to be out."

Hunter's dislike for the man grew with each slip of Abby's tongue. A pretty big feat, given he'd disliked the man intensely upon sight.

Abby turned around and leaned back against the rampart. Faced with a perfect shot, Hunter did what he did best. Let life play out on the other side of his lens.

"Did you just take my picture?" she asked when the shutter clicked.

"I've taken a lot of pictures."

"Well, stop." She averted her face, killing his view. "You know I don't like it."

"But I told you I'd photograph you again."

"And you pick another day when I don't have makeup on and I'm pale as a ghost."

"I don't want you made up. I prefer you the way you are." To prove his point, he pressed the shutter, despite her turned head.

"Now you're just being obnoxious," she murmured.

"No. I'm taking pictures. Not my fault you're a good model." He could practically hear her silent scoff. "You don't believe me?"

"Oh, I believe you," she replied, glancing over her shoulder. "The term *model* might be an exaggeration."

"Why are you so hard on the way you look?"

"Because I'm female," she replied with a smirk.

He didn't buy the answer, not for a second, and so he waited to speak again.

"I hate when you stare like that," she said.

"Stare how?"

"I don't like how you turn my comments into questions, either. You know what I'm talking about. The way you stare like you're looking through me."

"Not through you," he replied, shaking his head. "At you. I wish you could see yourself the way my camera does."

Abby curled the hair around her ear. "Unfortunately, your camera doesn't speak, and it hasn't spent twenty-five years telling me how average and unappealing I am."

God, but he really hated Warren now. Her parents, too, if they'd helped fill her head with such ragtime. "You're wrong," he said. "My camera does speak. I make it speak with what I see through my lens." Ignoring the doubt in her eyes, he moved a little closer. Perhaps if he showed her in the viewfinder the scenes he'd been photographing... "And what my camera says is that you are a woman of strength and character who has really amazing hair."

She smiled a little at the last part. "Amazing hair, huh?"

"Fantastic hair. Like a lion's mane," Hunter said, smiling back.

He meant to show her. He meant to hold out the camera so she could see for herself. Instead, their eyes caught and his intentions fell away. Everything fell away. The pavilion, the crowd, the violinist. All he could see was Abby. Her pale, unmade-up face, her shining eyes. A piece of hair blew across her cheek, the end clinging to her lower lip. Lucky strand.

He reached out and brushed the hair free, letting his fingers linger at the corner of her mouth.

"Your skin's cold," he said.

"Sun's going down. Guess Indian summer's all over. Time to return to reality." As she said the last part, she ducked her head, breaking contact with his touch. Not, however, before he caught the note of regret she was trying to hide.

"Not yet," he told her. "Come with me."

CHAPTER SIX

SHE MAY HAVE given up princess fantasies, but Abby had to admit she was starting to feel a little royal today. And her mood had nothing to do with visiting Belvedere Castle. Not at all. It was the look she saw on Hunter's face. He'd told her last night that he kept his subjects at an emotional distance, but standing there, stroking the hair from her cheek, the way his eyes held hers made her feel…special. Beautiful.

Must be what photographers did to charm models.

Even so, her lips continued to tingle from his touch as he led her back through the park and across the street. As she stepped inside the tavern, she felt she'd traded one castle for another, only this one was far more intimate. The narrow space was a honeycomb of velvet sofas and candlelit nooks warmed by a giant fireplace. Because it was only midafternoon, the establishment was empty except for a few couples tucked in dark corners. The emptiness only added to the romance, making it feel as though Hunter had brought her to his own private hideaway.

Abby brushed the hair from her face. Lion's mane or not, between the wind and her tumble, her hair had to look more of a tangled mess than usual. Way too messy for a place like this.

The hostess led them to a seat in front of the main fireplace. "This is amazing," Abby said as they settled on velvet cushions. Even though the fireplace was off on such a warm day, she could imagine the warmth.

"I come here to unwind sometimes," Hunter replied, sliding into the seat next to her. "Reminds me of a place in London."

"I can imagine. The unwinding, that is." She decided curling into the sofa would be uncouth, and settled for crossing her legs and sitting back against the pillows. "I walked by this place a few times when heading to the park, and always thought it was some kind of private club." Or maybe the upscale atmosphere just felt off-limits to her. "Not that I would have gone in, anyway," she added.

"Why not?"

"Stopping off somewhere for a drink? Oh,

yeah, that would have gone over real well. Coming home with liquor on my breath."

Hunter turned so he could face her. Abby noticed he didn't have a problem tucking a leg beneath his body. "Let me guess, Warren had a double standard when it came to drinking."

"Warren had a double standard when it came to lots of things. Drinking, outside friends. Money. Took me almost a year of overstocking the pantry so he wouldn't notice when I began skimming off the grocery money."

It wasn't until she said it that she realized how much her simple comment revealed.

Hunter looked astonished. "I had no idea," he said.

"Hey, we do what we have to do." She waved a hand dismissively. To think about all she'd had to do to escape only reinforced how bad she'd let the situation become.

"But to plan for a year for walking away..."

"I wanted to be prepared. Coming to New York with Warren was a hasty decision, and look how good that turned out. Figured this time I'd 'repent in leisure,' as they say." Plus, if she were to be completely honest, it had taken her a while to work up the nerve, as well.

"Somehow I don't think leaving an abusive

boyfriend is quite what the phrase means," Hunter noted.

She shrugged. "Repent, regret—same thing."

The quirk of his brow said otherwise. Fortunately, the waitress arrived then, cutting short any comment, and he turned his attention to ordering.

"Do you mind?" he asked, indicating the menu.

"Be my guest." It was, she realized, the second time he'd taken charge like this. Part of her considered balking at the high-handedness. She was, after all, perfectly capable of reading a wine list. However, as in the Indian restaurant, Hunter clearly knew more about the contents than she. Besides, he asked, whereas Warren would have taken over without a word.

"Impressive," she remarked once the waitress departed with their order. Although not surprising, considering his background. A family who could afford a private chef no doubt held food—and drink—in high esteem. "Did you learn about wine from your father or the infamous Reynaldo?"

"Neither. I learned from a bed-and-breakfast owner in Napa Valley. I was photographing a wine festival, and she offered to help me with my research."

"She. So, we're back to the little black book then."

"What makes you think she's in my book?"

"Is she?"

His smile said yes; Abby decided she didn't like the woman.

"Reynaldo was a lousy cook," Hunter said a beat later. He'd gone back to fiddling with his camera, twisting and popping off the lens cap, then putting it back on again. "Used to burn the macaroni and cheese."

"Doesn't sound like much of a private chef."

"That's because he wasn't a chef. I'm not even sure he had proper training. But then—" he gave Abby a strange smile "—my mother didn't hire him for his cooking."

"I don't understand…" Abby dragged out the sentence. Surely Hunter wasn't suggesting what she thought he was suggesting? Didn't he say his mother had been sick?

"He made her laugh," Hunter replied, and Abby gave a silent sigh of relief. For whatever reason, she didn't like the idea of Hunter's mother having an affair with the help while her son ate alone. "He'd flirt and say these outrageous things to her, like calling her 'Senora Seximama.' Stupid, I know, but she giggled every time."

His eye roll had a wistful affection to it. "I think that's what I remember most. Her laugh.

"Anyway," he continued, "I think she hired Reynaldo more for comic relief than the food."

"Your father didn't mind?"

"My father laughed with her. The two of them laughed together a lot before..."

Suddenly interested in the lens cap again, he let the sentence trail off. Finishing wasn't necessary. Abby heard enough sadness in the words Hunter did say. It was a different despair than when he'd told her about Somalia. It was a deeper sadness. A lonely sadness. Coupled with a resignation that came from carrying the burden around for a long time.

Abby hated to think she understood, but she did. Not losing a parent—the parent would have to stick around for you to lose them. But the deep-seated feeling of loss in general—that she understood too well.

She wanted to reach out and squeeze his hand, but the moment shifted before she had the chance. Their server arrived, discreetly setting their drinks on the table.

Hunter handed Abby a glass. "You know, you never said where you lived before moving to New York."

Changing the subject. Abby could understand that, as well. "Schenectady," she answered.

"Ever think of going back?"

"What for? My parents?" She shook her head. "Maybe, if it was only my mother, but as long as my stepfather is around, no way. I'd rather live on the streets." Nearly damn near did.

"A bad guy, is he?"

"Remember when I told you my mother and I both had bad taste in men?"

Hunter nodded.

"Mine's the better of the two. At least I can blame being too young to know better. Mom? I don't know what her reason, other than she didn't learn her lesson the first time." Abby plucked at the piping on the sofa arm. Who knew what drove her mother to cling to the jerk? Fear of being alone? "He was the reason I ran off with Warren after graduation."

"Did he—"

"Oh, no!" She shook her head. Aaron was a bully, but he wasn't a monster, thank goodness. "You know that phrase 'spare the rod'? He was a big believer. Particularly when I messed up, or mouthed off." Or caught his eye on a bad day. "Lucky for me, I got used to his moods. A good skill to have. Came in pretty handy during the Warren years."

"Not every man requires you to spend your time walking on eggshells, Abby."

She knew he'd say something like that. "So the counselors tell me."

"They're right."

"Maybe." Whether they were or not didn't matter; she didn't plan to test their theory by becoming emotionally involved again.

She sipped her wine. The dark red liquid was rich and dry. "Listen to us, will you? Last night I said we didn't have to go tit for tat, but here we are, swapping sad stories. First Reynaldo, then my stepfather."

It took only a swallow for the wine to seep into her veins, melting away a chill she didn't know she had. "I don't know about you, but I'm tired of being depressing. It's too beautiful a day. I'd much rather exchange happy stories."

"Such as?"

"Such as is there anywhere in the world you'd like to visit but haven't yet?"

"Schenectady."

She nudged his ankle with her toe. "Seriously. Where would you go?"

"Good question." Abby took another sip while he appeared to give the question real thought—a first for any man in her life. "I've never been to Antarctica," he said.

Not the answer she would have guessed. "You want to go to the South Pole?"

"Why not? In one of my father's photography books I remember seeing photos of Shackleton's ship, the *Endurance*. He ran aground there in the early twentieth century. The contrast of the white icebergs against the gray sky was so bleak, yet powerful. I'd love to do a modern black-and-white study."

"I have to admit, taking photographs of icebergs would not be my idea of a dream trip." Although she'd gladly listen to him talk about the project if it meant watching his face brighten. Whenever he spoke about his craft, he grew animated. The enthusiasm brought out the blue in his eyes, reminding Abby of dark water. She liked the color on him. She liked the brightness.

Maybe it was the wine, but she suddenly felt warm in a whole bunch of places deep inside her.

Hunter, meanwhile, had shifted in his seat so he was leaning closer. "All right, smarty-pants, where would you go?"

"Europe," she replied. She didn't need to think twice.

"Anywhere in particular? Or just Europe as a whole?"

"I've always wanted to go to Paris."

"Maybe someday you will."

Sure. She was still earning the down payment for an apartment. "Today I'll settle for having seen a little more of New York. Six years here, and I feel like I haven't seen anything." Hadn't lived much, either.

Someone had turned on the sound system, adding soft jazz music to the atmosphere. Abby drained her glass and sighed. The heat was beginning to spread through her limbs. She was relaxed and melty-feeling. "Today has been really nice," she told him. "Thank you."

"You're welcome." He was looking at her in that way again. Zeroing in on her as if there was nothing else to focus on. In her new relaxed state, she found herself noticing new details about her employer. Like the way the hair curled about the tops of his ears, and the regal slope of his nose. Long and graceful. Like the way he moved.

She noticed his hands, too. How they were large and capable, yet cradled the base of his goblet with gentleness. She'd watched how those hands treated his camera the same way. The touch never too hard or too soft, but always—always—with assuredness.

Heat changed to an ache. Desire, Abby realized. The feeling curled long and low inside her. With one look he made her feel like more of a woman than Warren had in six years. No way that little black book of Hunter's was anything short of a mile thick. Not with that skill.

He believed in keeping the world at arm's length. No commitment; no false promises. No strings, demands or control.

Last night she'd questioned his rules, thought they were wrong for him, but now the idea of emotional distance sounded just about right.

Just about right indeed.

His lips were dark and shining from the wine. "Something on your mind?" he asked.

"I was thinking about dinner," she replied. "Be a shame for you to fly to the Middle East tomorrow without one last home-cooked meal."

She shifted in her seat, closing the distance to less than a foot. If Hunter noticed her new proximity, he didn't seem to mind. In fact, he set his goblet down and moved in a hair closer.

"We've been through this," he said. "You don't have to cook me dinner."

He brushed his knuckles along her cheek, causing a thrill to run through her. "I don't expect you to wait on me hand and foot."

If she had any doubts about what she wanted, those magic words blew them away. They, along with his gentle touch, turned her bold. Tomorrow, he would be overseas. Why not give herself tonight?

"Then I won't cook," she said in a soft voice. She couldn't help it; her eyes had to look at his mouth again. "How about I just keep you company instead?"

She kissed him.

At first he did what any man would do. He kissed her back. Hunter opened his mouth and drank her in, savoring her taste and texture. He heard her sigh, and he kissed her even deeper as her fingers twisted in his jacket, pulling their bodies closer together, oblivious to their surroundings. That is, until his foot nudged the table leg.

What the hell was he doing?

This wasn't some woman. This was Abby, who'd spent the afternoon telling him about shattered fairy tales, and who was laden down with baggage. Gripping her shoulders, he reluctantly pulled himself back from the embrace. "I can't…"

"Ohmygod!"

There was no need to finish. Slapping a hand to her mouth, she shot to her feet, em-

barrassment and confusion turning her eyes
black. "How about we pretend that never happened, okay? Turn back the clock, act like
we never left the apartment. I mean, never…
Never mind. I'm going to leave now."

"Hold on." This was not how he wanted to
leave town. With the picture of her looking so
wounded stuck in his head. He tossed a few
bills on the table and caught up with her by
the front entrance.

"It's not that I'm not flattered. It's just that—"

"Don't." She silenced him with both hands.
"Please spare me the 'it's not you, it's me'
speech. I've had a crappy enough week as
it is."

A lousy week because of him. He could
kick himself for not stopping her when he'd
seen her leaning toward him. He knew exactly what she was thinking, and he hadn't
done a thing.

*Because you were thinking the exact same
thing. You wanted to kiss her.* God, but did
he want to kiss her.

Least he could do was apologize. He
moved to lay a hand on her shoulder, but she
shrugged off his touch. Arms folded, she
stood staring at the street outside, the barriers
firmly in place. "We should be heading back
to your apartment. I left my pocketbook there.

"Besides," she added in a stiff voice, "I'm sure you have a lot to do before you leave town. Packing. Getting takeout."

Abby shoved open the door. Too bad it didn't have a proper hinge so she could slam it behind her. Block Hunter and the memory of what happened. She knew she'd screwed up the second Hunter's hands had gripped her shoulders. What an idiot. Thinking Hunter, who could have any woman he wanted, would add her to his list.

So much for being amazing. Oh wait, it was her hair Hunter called amazing. What was she, again? Regrettable, apparently. Oh, and baggage laden. She couldn't forget the baggage. After all, Hunter clearly hadn't.

She wished she'd never agreed to take the stupid walk with him. Now she was stuck walking back, too. A couple miles of awkward silence. The only reason she was returning to his apartment was because she needed her pocketbook. Otherwise she'd jump on the nearest subway. Disappearing into a hole sounded awfully good about now.

"I should explain," he said about a half mile in.

Oh no, he was going to apologize again. She'd rather the silence. "You don't have to."

"I want to. You're an attractive woman, Abby, but kissing you…kissing you was a mistake."

"Really? Never would have guessed."

Hunter winced. *Good,* thought Abby. He deserved to feel a little more stupid.

"What I'm trying to say is that I'm… That is, I…" He took a deep breath, presumably to start again. "You deserve better."

"Better than what?"

"Than a guy taking off for the West Bank in a few hours."

"Oh." So that was it. He'd heard her talking about fairy tales and princes this afternoon, and he'd assumed that's what she was looking for. She grabbed his arm.

"No offense, but what makes you think you know what I deserve?" Rejecting her was one thing, but who was he to make assumptions? She was going to set him straight right now. "You better than anyone know that I just got out of the relationship from hell. Did you ever stop to think I might not want more than a few hours?"

"That's not who you are."

Says who? Him? "Excuse me, but you don't know who I am," she snapped. "And you sure as hell don't get to decide whether I'm looking for a fling. Six years having my life dictated is enough, thank you very much."

"Fine. Next time we make out, I'll ask before I stop kissing you. Okay?"

"Thank you." She tried to keep the flutter that erupted at the words *next time* under control.

CHAPTER SEVEN

"Got your coffee, I see."

It was two weeks later, and Abby and Hunter were having their regular video chat. Originally, when they'd said their uncomfortable goodbyes, Hunter said he would check in "once or twice" to see if she needed anything. Once or twice, it turned out, meant daily. In a way, talking regularly was a good thing. It helped them get over the awkward hump left behind after their kiss.

You mean after you threw yourself at him.

It probably also helped that they'd come to some silent, mutual decision to pretend the kiss had never happened. If Abby every once in a while felt a flash of heat when cleaning Hunter's bedroom, or experienced a passing, random memory of how good his lips felt… well, she quickly shoved the thoughts aside. No point dwelling on the embarrassing. Even if it was the best kiss she'd ever experienced.

Despite her resolve, however, there was one nagging thought she couldn't shake: for a brief moment, Hunter had kissed her back. More than kissed. *Kissed.*

Originally, after the disaster in the wine bar, she'd briefly considered quitting. In fact, she'd rehearsed her speech on the trip back from the bar. Nothing else to do, since neither of them were talking to each other. Before she could say a word, however, Hunter had surprised her by shoving his door key in her hand.

"You still want me?" Abby had immediately asked. "I mean, as a housekeeper?"

"I promised you temporary work until you got back on your feet. I see no reason why I shouldn't keep that promise. Do you?"

Actually, Abby could have given several, but in the end, he was leaving town and she needed money, so she stayed quiet.

Which was why she now sat in front of a computer monitor with a coffee mug cradled between her hands, while across the ocean Hunter did the same with a glass of beer.

"Don't know why you're so surprised," she said, when they were finishing up their morning chat. "These calls of yours are the perfect excuse for a coffee break." To illustrate her point, she took a large swallow, while in the back of her mind she wondered if the reason they both brought drinks was to keep their hands occupied while they talked. Empty hands led to fidgeting, and fidgeting would reveal the awkwardness they were both trying to hide.

"Did you get the package I sent you?" she asked, raising the cup to her lips again.

"Waiting downstairs when I checked out."

"Good. I was afraid the protests would delay delivery."

"You needn't have been concerned," Hunter said over his beer. Today's selection was a dark-looking ale. "Protests are several miles away from the hotel."

Maybe so, but Hunter had been in the middle of them. Abby hadn't forgotten his cavalier attitude toward his personal safety. He might not care what happened to himself, but someone should. For now, the task fell to her. She owed him. After all, he did step in to help her. She'd spent the week scanning the internet and news reports to keep abreast of the action.

Which reminded her. "I saw one of your photos online yesterday."

"How'd it look?"

Thinking of it, she shivered. "Violent. Bloody."

On his side of the computer screen, Hunter nodded, and she knew he was remembering which shot. "How's everything else?"

"Good. I bought you a plant to green up your windowsill. For a photographer, you have surprisingly bland walls."

"I meant the job hunt."

"Oh, right, that." She set down her cup, the coffee having turned sour-tasting. "Going."

"Didn't you have an interview this week?"

He would remember. "I did. They hired someone with more experience."

"Happens."

A lot. In fact, it had become a pattern. Every morning she circled want ads and filled out applications, only to hear she either didn't have enough experience or the job had been filled before she got there. The other day, she'd lost out to the woman who showed up fifteen minutes before her.

What bothered Abby most, however, wasn't losing out on the job. It was the fact that none of them appealed to her. Surely her fresh start meant more than waiting tables or answering phones? For crying out loud, she'd gotten more satisfaction from buying Hunter his plant.

That fact might bother her most of all.

"Abby?"

She blinked. "I'm sorry."

"I said my flight gets in at seven-thirty. Could you call the car company and confirm the reservation?"

"Sure. Of course." She scribbled a reminder note, and told herself the flurry of emotions in her chest was embarrassment. "Bet you're looking forward to coming home."

"It's only a quick stopover. I take off again at the end of the week."

"Well, with luck I'll be out of your hair before you leave. I mean—" she glanced up "—luck can change, right?"

There must have been a flicker in the connection, because as she was looking up from her notepad, it appeared as if his expression slipped. However, on second look, his face was the same as always, handsome and impassive. "With luck," he repeated.

His words sounded flat.

They spoke for a few more minutes, mostly about travel arrangements, before Hunter told her he had to sign off. "I won't have a chance to check in tomorrow morning," he told her.

"You'll see me tomorrow night."

"You don't have to stick around. I have no idea how long it will take getting back from the airport."

"That's all right, I don't mind waiting for

you." Realizing how her comment might come across, especially after their kiss, she scrambled to add, "You forget, tomorrow's payday. Even temporary employees get paid."

"Yes, they do," he said with, unless she was mistaken, a little bit of relief in his voice. "I'll see you tomorrow night, Abby."

"Hunter?" She caught him as he was reaching to sign off. "Be safe."

He gave a quick nod, and the screen went blank.

Hunter jogged up the stairs to his apartment. He must have slept better on the plane than he thought. Normally international flights left him drained.

Could also be that the drive from the airport took less time than usual. He'd have to thank Abby for double-checking the reservation.

Abby. As he rounded the second floor landing, the smile her name brought to his face faded. He'd been thinking about her, or rather their arrangement, a lot this trip. Wondering if he hadn't made a mistake offering her a temporary job. Granted, she appeared to be doing well, but the whole reason he'd made the offer was to ease his guilty conscience, and thus far he wasn't feeling less guilty at all. If anything, he felt worse.

That's what happens when you slip up and kiss someone you shouldn't. Problem was he didn't know if he felt guilty for kissing her or because he didn't have nearly the amount of regret he should have over the incident. If he concentrated, he could still taste her when he licked his lips. Her uniquely Abbyish taste.

Damn, he never had scratched that itch. God knew he'd tried to, but with every woman who crossed his path, he found himself comparing her mouth to Abby's or her dark hair to Abby's butterscotch curls. In the end, it was easier to sleep alone.

The apartment was dark and empty when he let himself in. "Abby?" He got a sinking sensation when he realized the apartment was empty. She'd said she'd be waiting for him.

Guess she got a better offer. *Did you ever stop to think I might not want more than a few hours?*

Unacceptable, he thought as he looked around the empty space. Completely unacceptable. Temporary hire or not, if she was going to change plans, she needed to let him know. A call, a note. Something. Grabbing his cell phone, he punched out the phone number she'd given him. *There'd better be a good ex-*

planation. What if he'd counted on her being here for business or…or some housekeeping emergency?

Abby answered on the fourth ring. "Hunter! You're back in New York!"

He ignored the rush he felt at her enthusiastic greeting. "Funny thing," he said in return. "My apartment's empty."

"Yeah, I know. I meant to be there when you got in, but something came up."

Something or someone? His jaw remained as stiff as his spine. "An emergency?"

"Sort of. I'm…" There was a pause, followed by the sound of muffled voices. Wherever she was, she wasn't alone.

"Abby? Where are you?" Hunter squeezed the phone as he waited for a response.

"I'm at the police station."

Hunter found Abby sitting on a bench in the precinct corridor. As soon as he saw her, the nausea that had been churning in his stomach since her phone call eased.

He called her name and she looked up with big brown eyes.

He rushed over to her. "What happened? Are you—" He looked her up and down for signs she'd been roughed up. Her hair hung in her face. He reached out to brush the strands aside.

"I'm fine," she said, backing away. It was a lie. There was a palm-size red mark on her cheek. His blood began to boil.

"Warren showed up where I live," she told him.

"I thought you made sure he didn't know where you lived?" Hunter didn't even know.

"I did. Apparently he went to the diner looking for me, and Guy suggested he check across the street."

The miserable old— Hunter was going to wring his scrawny neck.

"Anyway…" She sat back down. He noticed she'd gone back to wearing her baggy cardigan, which she now pulled tight. "Anyway, he must have seen me coming out of your building, and followed me home. He cornered me by the subway stop this morning and wanted me to get in his car and go somewhere to talk. I managed to get away and head back to the house. We've been tied up with police stuff ever since."

"We?"

"My friend Carmella. She came with me. She's in the ladies' room freshening up. Been a long day, to say the least." Heaving a sigh, Abby swiped the hair from her face, the very hair Hunter had reached for earlier. When she looked at him again, he saw that her eyes were overly bright and shining. "I'm sorry I wasn't at the apartment like I promised," she said.

"Not a big deal. Obviously you had a reason." Looking back, he felt like a heel for overreacting the way he had. Especially now that he had a clear view of the mark marring her cheek.

"Does it hurt?" He tried to look closer, but she quickly shook her head, bringing the hair back into her face. "I meant to leave a message letting you know what happened, but then we got tied up with statements and filling out forms."

"It's all right."

"I said I'd cook dinner, too. You're probably starved. As soon as we're done—"

"Abby, I said it's all right." The words came out sharper than he meant them to.

She pulled her sweater even tighter. "It won't happen again."

"I'm sure it won't." Although he appreciated the promise, her comeback sounded wrong. It lacked her usual sharpness.

The flight was catching up with him. Stifling a yawn, he sat down on the bench next to her, only to have her scoot a foot in the opposite direction. About ten inches more than she needed to. That's when he finally caught the fearful look in her eyes.

"Hey." Making sure his voice was as soft and gentle as possible, he shifted so he could look her in the eye. "You know I'm not Warren, right?"

"Of course," she replied. There was too much defensiveness in her voice, however, to sound very convincing.

Dammit, now he really hated himself for sounding so harsh on the phone. Must have scared the daylights out her. Worse, he had absolutely no good explanation for why he'd gotten so upset.

None of that mattered at the moment, however. He needed to reassure Abby.

Poor thing looked worn-out. With the exception of Warren's ugly reminder, her skin had turned pale as powder. The mouth that he'd found amazingly kissable only two weeks before was a colorless line. He wished he could run his thumb across the surface and bring the color back.

"Are you sure?" He wanted to be absolutely certain she understood that he was nothing like her ex-boyfriend. It had suddenly become very important she know that. "Are you really sure? Because while I might lose my temper, I would never hurt you. You know that, right?"

Giving in to the impulse to touch her, he covered her hand with his, relaxing when she didn't flinch and pull away. "I believe you," she said with a sad smile.

Relief spread through Hunter's chest.

He coughed to clear the sudden tightness. "So is Warren under arrest?"

"They're going to talk to the prosecutor."

"Which is a total joke," a strange voice boomed. A short African-American woman, whose build definitely didn't fit her voice, walked toward them. Carmella, he presumed.

"It's up to the lawyers to decide if there's enough evidence to do anything."

"Problem is I don't have any evidence or witnesses," Abby said.

"What do they call that mark on your cheek? Chopped liver?"

Hunter agreed. "Don't forget, you had a restraining order. You told me he skipped the hearing last week. Doesn't that mean the order is still in effect?"

Both Abby and Carmella looked at him with jaded expressions. "Again," Carmella said, "no witnesses. He can lie through his teeth."

"Probably will, too. God, I feel so stupid."

Abby buried her face in her hands. "I actually thought that once I left, he'd forget about me."

"It's not your fault the guy's a jerk," Carmella said.

"So people keep telling me. I'm just tired of the whole thing."

It killed Hunter to hear the defeat in Abby's voice. This wasn't the woman whose photo he'd taken outside the diner.

"Problem is," Carmella said, "you're exhausted. A good night's sleep and everything will seem brighter."

"Hope your right," Abby said with a sigh. "Lord knows, I am beat." She looked to him. "We may be stuck here for a while."

In other words, she was offering him an out to go back to the apartment. His reluctance to leave her outweighed any exhaustion he was feeling. "I already came across town to get here. Might as well wait till you're finished."

A hint of a smile curled her lips, the first positive sign he'd seen since arriving. Though only a small thing, seeing it made him happy. "You said that last time, when we spent the day at the courthouse."

"What can I say? I like hanging in municipal buildings with you," he told her. "Why don't you and your friend find out what's happening? I'll call a car and catch up with you."

"Seriously, Hunter, there's no need for you to—"

He held up a finger to stop the protest. "I need a ride home, anyway. Might as well travel in style. Now go."

"That's the photographer, huh?" Carmella asked as they walked back to the squad room.

"That's him."

"I can see why you took the job. Guy looks like a movie star."

"I took the job because I need the money," Abby replied. "Besides, the job's only temporary. He threw me a bone because he felt guilty over getting me fired from the diner."

"And did his guilt or the bone make him come all the way over here?"

"I'm not in the mood." Abby wasn't really upset. Her friend was only trying to lighten the mood.

She still couldn't believe Warren showing up the way he had. He'd been as unreasonable as ever, spewing angry comments about her and Hunter. *You really think a guy like that is going to let you stick around? You're just a bed warmer.* Had she not been focused on getting away, she might have told Warren his rantings were not just irrational, but completely impossible.

"You didn't answer my question," Carmella pointed out.

Abby wasn't sure she had an answer. Why had Hunter ridden all the way across town? To check on her? There were men who did things like that simply because they were decent people. Hadn't Hunter said his Southerner mother had taught him manners?

"I assume he came because he was worried. He knows what Warren's capable of, so when I told him I was at the police station, he got concerned."

"Uh-huh. My boss wouldn't drive across town to check up on me."

Her implication was obvious. In spite of everything that had happened, Abby had to roll her eyes in amusement. "For crying out loud, I'm at the station house filing charges against my ex-boyfriend. What on earth made you think I'm even interested in Hunter Smith?"

"I don't know. Maybe because he's hot and rich?"

And off-limits, Abby added silently. Which was a good thing. Not that she was interested in men at the moment—one look at her surroundings was confirmation enough of that point—but if she were to someday return to the dating scene, it wouldn't be with a man as overwhelming as Hunter. In retrospect, it was a good thing that he turned her down. If the way her insides leapt at the sight of him was any indication, a fling would have been a bad idea.

"Unfortunately, since it's your word against his, there's not a lot we can do," the officer told her.

"In other words, her ex can just do anything he wants." Carmella shook her head.

"He can't do anything," the officer replied. "If we catch him breaking the order, we can arrest him. But without firm evidence…"

"There's nothing you can do," Abby finished for him. This was great. When was she going to catch a break?

"Isn't there anything more you can do?"

Abby started at the sound of Hunter's voice. She hadn't heard him join them. Turning around, she saw him hovering over her like a big protective bird. Too bad he wasn't really an action hero.

"We're doing everything we can," the officer replied. He seemed to sit up straighter before addressing Hunter's concern. "We've reminded Mr. Pelligini what will happen if he steps out of line. And we'll have a patrol car keep an eye on McKenzie House. That way, if he shows up again, we can act immediately."

Abby nodded. Wasn't much, but it was something. "Thanks."

"Wish we could do more, ma'am."

Yeah, she did, too.

"I can't believe this," Carmella said when they left the squad room. "We spend all day here and the best they can do is to keep an eye on the house?"

No sense pointing out the fact that both she and Carmella had predicted the outcome. "There's only so much they can do, without proof. Maybe we'll get lucky and Warren will do something stupid."

Carmella scoffed. "What are you supposed to do in the meantime? Lock yourself in the house?"

"I could always stay at a hotel." So much for her apartment nest egg. Still, she'd certainly sleep better in a new location. "Maybe the desk officer can recommend a place that's not too expensive."

"You're not staying at a hotel."

Again, Hunter's voice startled her. Up to that moment, he'd been unusually quiet. Regretting ever meeting her, Abby assumed. Lord knew, she would. "Where would I stay, then? Because I truly don't want to sleep at home tonight."

His expression was as unreadable as ever

when he looked over at her. Didn't matter, because his words caused her heart to skitter. "My place," he said. "You'll come stay with me."

CHAPTER EIGHT

"No way." Abby shook her head.

"Why not?" Hunter looked at her as if she had two heads. "It's the perfect solution. I have a second bedroom. State-of-the-art security. You would be going back and forth to my place for work, anyway. This way you won't have to worry about running into Warren while you're commuting."

"Makes a lot a sense to me," Carmella said.

Perfect sense. But Abby's gut said it was a horrible idea. "The whole reason Warren flipped out was because he saw me at your place," she told Hunter. "What's he going to do if he finds out I'm sleeping there? He'll go even crazier."

"I hate to break it to you, sweetheart, but Warren's going to think what he thinks no matter what you do."

True enough. When they were going out, Warren had constantly accused her of con-

spiracies, from shrinking his clothes to pur-
posely forgetting his favorite foods to "hurt"
him. If he thought she was involved with
Hunter, nothing would change his mind. But
to sleep in the same apartment as Hunter?
His essence was all over that place. Surely
that wouldn't help ease her rest. It definitely
wouldn't help her attraction. Just thinking
about the arrangement sent her pulse into
overdrive.

"I'll be fine at McKenzie House," she
told them both. "There are plenty of people
around. The police will be patrolling—"

Hunter cut her off. "This isn't up for debate, Abby."

What? Of course it was up for debate. She
was the victim, for crying out loud. Who did
he think he was? She looked to Carmella for
support. Her friend merely shrugged. "Sorry,
I think he's right."

Unbelievable. She was being bullied into
where she should hide from a bully.

An hour later, still angry at being forced
into the arrangement, Abby headed downstairs. Her plan was to make one last argument. Instead, she got to the third step from
the bottom and found Hunter sprawled across
his living room sofa, his long frame illuminated by the computer screen. While she'd

been upstairs fuming, he'd changed into a pair of track pants and an unzipped sweatshirt. She paused, struck by how different he looked in the moment. Stripped of his action-hero uniform, with his hair mussed and his attention stolen, the vulnerability he normally kept barricaded seeped out. This was a softer, gentler Hunter. His lips were parted in concentration.

Noticing how his eyes picked up the gleam of the computer screen, she wondered, if she were closer, would she see the computer image reflected in their blue-gray depths? This was a different Hunter. The one he showed only glimpses of. Her heart jumped to her throat, killing her irritation. This was why she'd argued against staying. How could she fight an attraction when she saw Hunter unguarded? Given what she'd been through today, she shouldn't be feeling any attraction at all toward anyone. Yet here she was, mesmerized by the man. Clearly, her self-destructive tendencies were alive and well.

She must have sighed or made some other noise because he looked up. "You're awake."

"So are you," she countered.

"Couldn't sleep, so I decided to answer a few emails. Thought you'd collapse the minute you went upstairs. It's not every day you get attacked by an ex-boyfriend."

"Just every three or four."

Surprisingly, the sarcasm earned a smile. "Nice to know you're back on form. Have you settled in?"

"Pretty much. It's not like I had a lot to unpack."

"You could have brought more."

"Didn't have much to begin with." She came down the rest of the stairs, joining him in the living space. He'd sat up while speaking, his sweatshirt falling open to reveal his bare chest. "There's coffee if you want some."

Abby had to smile. "Someone finally used his coffeemaker."

"What can I say? Someone stocked my pantry with coffee."

Padding to the kitchen area, she poured herself a cup, while Hunter sat up and cleared room for her to sit. It felt strange being in his house this late at night. She wondered how he felt about his space being invaded, he who spent so much of his time alone.

"Thank you letting me stay."

"Wasn't about to let you go home and risk getting beat up," he replied.

"A hotel would have worked just as well."

"Right. I would have felt real good about

dropping you off somewhere in your price range."

Abby joined him on the sofa. "I wouldn't have minded."

"I know. Sadly." He picked up his coffee cup, started to drink, then set it back down again. "This isn't a punishment, Abby. Even your friend thought staying here was a good idea."

Because her *friend* was as bad as Warren when it came to thinking something was going on between the two of them. Hunter was right, though. Most people would be thrilled by his generosity. "I'm sorry. I don't mean to sound ungrateful. I was being a brat."

"I wish you'd stop apologizing."

"Sorry for that, too." Before he could open his mouth to lecture, she grinned to let him know she was joking. He mock-glared back.

"Why did you argue the point?" he asked.

"I think you know."

"My kissing you."

Hearing him say the words aloud brought the memory shooting to the surface. Remembering brought a sigh to her lips, and she had to bite down to keep the sound from escaping. "I kissed you, if I recall."

"We kissed each other, and I also recall us settling things."

Oh yes, they'd settled things. To a point. "I was afraid it might be…awkward."

Hunter studied the contents of his coffee cup. "We've been talking over the internet for the past two weeks. Are you saying you're still thinking about what happened?"

"No," she quickly assured him. "What I meant was we haven't seen each other in person since that happened. It's one thing to communicate by computer, but when you're in the same room…"

"My personality hasn't changed, Abby, if that's what you're wondering."

"Never would have guessed."

Setting deeper into the corner, Abby sipped her coffee and thought about how intertwined hers and Hunter's lives had become the past few weeks. The level to which he had ended up involved. A lot for a guy who preferred to be on the sidelines capturing the action. She could only imagine his regret. "I bet you're sorry you ever sat in my section of the diner, aren't you?"

"Why do you say that?"

Wasn't it obvious? "I've been nothing but trouble from the start. Since meeting me you've been kicked out of your favorite break-fast place, hired a housekeeper you didn't want, been arrested for assault—"

"My lawyer assures me the charges will go away," he interrupted.

Still, he faced the hassle of fighting the charges in the first place. "And now you're stuck with a roommate on your first night back from overseas."

For a moment, Hunter didn't reply. Then he slid a little closer. "My apartment needed cleaning," he said. The simple response made her vision blur.

"I'm sorry for messing up your life," she said, blinking.

"You don't have to apologize."

"Maybe I want to." Over the years, she'd given so many apologies simply to avoid conflict. It felt good to give one on her terms.

To her relief, he understood. At least that's how she chose to interpret his nod. "Apology accepted then."

She suddenly had to blink again.

Silence settled between them. Tucking herself in the corner of the sofa, Abby sipped her coffee and tried not to think about how intimate the setting felt. The computer screen cast no more light than a candle, and with Hunter only a foot away, she became acutely aware of his presence. Every breath, every rasp of cotton against his skin, every gap in his open sweatshirt. Especially every gap in his sweatshirt. Despite the shadows, she could see every contour of his sculpted torso. He must have taken a shower, for with each breath, his skin gave off the faintest aroma of soap. The scent mingled with Italian roast to create a unique aftershave that instantly reminded her of how it felt to be wrapped in his arms.

Interestingly, it wasn't the kiss that popped to her mind, but the other embrace. When he'd held her during her meltdown, surrounding her with calm and security.

Next to her, she felt Hunter shift his weight. He was facing her. "I was thinking. About you being my housekeeper. There's no need for you to keep looking for work."

Abby had to pause to make sure she'd heard right. "I thought you said the arrangement could only be temporary."

"Those were the terms you offered me. You're a lousy negotiator."

He was offering her a full-time job. "Why?"

"I just told you why. I need my house clean."

He'd needed his house clean before he'd gone away, and had seemed in no hurry to have a full-time employee. She could think of only one reason for this new offer. "Your change of heart wouldn't have anything to do with Warren's reappearance today, would it?"

"What if it did?"

"At least you're honest."

"Look…" He slid across the leather until they were knee to knee. "Does it matter why I'm offering? You're not having luck finding another job, anyway, so why not? It'll help you get back on your feet that much faster."

True on all counts. Problem was, it did matter. She didn't want Hunter to see her as some charity case who needed help; he'd seen her that way enough. She wanted him to see her as…

As what? A woman? The notion stirred awareness deep inside her.

And if he looked at her that way? What then? She hung her head. Stress and exhaustion had her thinking in circles. Hunter was right about one thing: she wasn't having any luck finding other work. Only a stubborn fool would reject his offer.

"A job and a night in a luxury apartment. A girl could do a lot worse."

"You're welcome. Glad to see you've stopped being stubborn."

Stubborn. That's what Warren called her when she didn't do what he wanted.

At the thought of Warren, Abby felt the

day finally catch up with her, and exhaustion pressed hard on her shoulders. She needed to turn in before she did or said something foolish.

"Good night, Abby," Hunter said when she stood up.

She offered him a smile. "Thanks again. For everything."

"You're welcome. Again. Oh, and, Abby?" His fingers caught hers. "Just so you know, the room is yours for as long as you need."

Her heart leaped to her throat again, killing her ability to speak. Too bad she couldn't say the same for the voice in her head telling her she'd just made a very bad decision.

Hunter watched until Abby's stocking feet disappeared up the stairs. What was he thinking? He barely stayed in the apartment. He didn't need a housekeeper, certainly not one full-time. And living here to boot. Granted, the living arrangement was temporary. But then again, that was how the job had started.

He ran a hand over his face. What the hell had happened?

His coffee was long cold. No matter. He drank the liquid anyway. By all rights he should be dead to the world in a bed, like Abby, but he couldn't shake the image of her sitting on the police bench, her color drained away, and worrying he was mad at her. *You're probably sorry you ever met me.* He hated hearing her say things like that. He hated that ex-boyfriend of hers for dredging up her insecurities. Couldn't stand the idea Abby thought so little of herself. She was better than that.

Would you listen to him? Hunter slammed down his coffee cup. He sounded so protective. Hell, he was *acting* protective. The woman was sleeping in his spare bedroom, for crying out loud! When had Abby gone from being some waitress he saw being hassled, to sleeping upstairs, with him downstairs worrying about her? So much so he'd offered her a job and told her she could stay as long as she liked? When did he start *caring?* He wasn't supposed to care.

The only thing compassion did was cause you to get burned. He turned off his laptop, plunging the area into darkness. Sitting back, he closed his eyes and waited for his emotional wall to rebuild itself. The wall that since childhood had kept him whole, shielding him from loneliness, betrayal, desertion. Brick by brick, he would build an invisible fortress until the outside world stopped affecting him.

Only this time, the walls refused to rise. At some point between landing at the airport and now, his insides had shifted. There was a breach in the protection buffeting his soul. Because when he closed his eyes, the only thing his mind could see was Abby.

Abby tiptoed down the stairs, trying to be as quiet as possible in case Hunter was still asleep. He wasn't. Just her luck, she found him awake and propped against the kitchen counter eating a toasted frozen waffle slathered with peanut butter. He smiled when he saw her, an unusually shy smile that he managed to make look sexy, and raked his free hand through his curls. "Morning, Sleeping Beauty."

Talk about your misnomers. It was her turn to rake a hand through the mess on top of her head. Most women were cursed with either limp bangs or unruly curls. She'd gotten both, meaning bed head was not her friend. "I didn't mean to sleep so late." Unfortunately, her thoughts had kept her awake long after she should have slipped unconscious. "If you give me five minutes, I'll make you breakfast."

"Already made." He licked a dab of peanut butter from his lower lip. Abby tried not to focus on the sheen his tongue left behind. She'd thought the one good thing to come out of her tossing and turning was that she'd woken up determined to keep her fantasies in check. Instead, rather than improve, the awkwardness felt as if it increased tenfold. Seeing Hunter in his sweatshirt only reminded her of last night's eerily intimate conversation in the dark.

"See you're becoming a regular barista, too," she said, noting the full pot of coffee.

"Had no choice. My housekeeper slept in.

"Relax," he added when she began to protest. "It was a joke. Should I bother asking if the bed was comfortable?"

"A lot better than the thing the shelter calls a bed, that's for sure." Realizing what she'd said, Abby winced. Up to now, Hunter hadn't commented on her living arrangements. A fact she had hoped meant he didn't know.

He was in the middle of pouring her coffee. "Did you say 'shelter'?"

So much for hoping. Abby nodded. "McKenzie House. It's part of a network of houses around the city for battered women." She waited for the inevitable reaction.

"Damn!" Hunter swore with disbelief. "Why didn't you say anything?"

For what? So he could look at her with greater pity in his eyes? "Do you drop where you live into everyday conversation?"

"No."

"Neither do I."

"But a shelter?"

"McKenzie House isn't a homeless shelter. Not really. It's more like a halfway house where women can stay while getting back on their feet.

"Look," she said, leaning against the counter. "I'm not ashamed of where I live." Her only shame was in letting her life become such a mess in the first place.

Hunter held out her coffee. "Fair enough. Although I'd like to point out you no longer live at McKenzie House, either."

"This arrangement is temporary. Soon as Warren backs off, I'll go back."

"We'll see."

What was that supposed to mean? She'd opened her mouth to ask when Hunter turned on his heel. "Before I forget."

His messenger bag lay on the dining room table. Striding over to it, he reached in and retrieved what looked like a yellow plastic shopping bag. "Here." He thrust the sack in his direction.

"For me?"

She pulled out a gold-and-coral-colored scarf. *He'd bought her a present?* "It's beautiful."

"I was shooting near the marketplace, and one of the vendors had a bunch of them. I figured I should buy something."

Tiny embroidered flowers danced across the linen material. Abby ran her fingers over the raised metallic thread. She couldn't remember a gift that didn't come with an apology.

Or an expectation. Her stomach twisted. Hunter's kindness. Would there be a price tag attached to that, as well? Did she want one?

Her thoughts must have played out on her face, because suddenly there was Hunter, closer than he should be, catching her chin with his fingers. Forcing her face upward, he met her gaze with a gentle seriousness. "It's only a scarf."

He was halfway upstairs before Abby found her ability to speak—too late for him to hear her whispered thank-you. She could kick herself for jumping to such a wrong conclusion. Then again, she was still seeing the world through her Warren-skewed lens. Goes to show, old habits die hard.

And old baggage never quite went away.

* * *

"I can't believe you don't have a single picture."

Hunter looked up from the shot he was editing. "I beg your pardon?"

"On your walls," Abby replied. "I can't believe they're bare. You're a photographer, for goodness' sake."

"Which means I'm required to hang photographs?" He was teasing her. She'd been muttering about photos and artwork for the past twenty minutes. so he knew exactly what she meant. He just enjoyed seeing her gear up for a discussion.

They'd been living together for three days. That is, Abby had been his live-in housekeeper for three days. With each tick of the calendar, she seemed to get more comfortable.

Personally, Hunter wasn't sure how he felt. Having spent the better part of his life alone, he was used to silence and solitude. Abby brought chatter and activity to his otherwise quiet workday, knocking him from his rhythm and interrupting his concentration.

On the other hand, she brought chatter and activity to his otherwise quiet workday. Suddenly he had noises in his kitchen, and conversation over dinner and...

And midday debates about whether his walls were too bare.

"You are planning to stay here while I'm in Libya, aren't you?" he asked. It was a question that had been bothering him since their arrangement began. There'd been no sign of Warren since she moved in, a fact that he knew hadn't escaped her notice.

"I was thinking about it, and decided I should go back to McKenzie House." A ridiculously small plant sat on the windowsill. She picked up the pot and carried it to the kitchen sink. "Why? Does that bother you?"

Did it? "Yes."

"Why? You won't be here. Besides, if I don't go back, they'll give away my spot."

"And would that be such a bad idea?" he asked her. "Is staying here so awful?"

"No. Of course not." A shadow crossed her face. She was holding part of her answer back. He wondered what. "Why do you care so much?"

Truthfully? He didn't know why he found her insistence on keeping one foot at the shelter bothersome. It shouldn't matter to him at all, or so his brain would tell him. It was his insides—his gut, his chest—that seemed to cramp up at the idea. All he knew was that when she talked of leaving, his nonthinking parts told him it was a bad idea.

"I think you should stay. You've got a bedroom. Going back only takes a bed away from someone else."

"I…" Clearly, she hadn't thought of that point. Mentioning it might have been underhanded if it weren't also true. If there was one thing Hunter had learned about Abby this week, it was that she believed strongly in McKenzie House's mission, and the people it helped.

He could tell the moment she acquiesced by the nervous darkness underscoring her expression. "Cheer up," he told her, trying not to be annoyed. "I'll be gone. You'll have a whole week to hang photos."

Surprise replaced the darkness. Her eyes grew wide. "While you're out of town?"

"Sure," he replied with a wave of his hand. "Hang away." If it would make her face light up like that, he'd let her knock down walls. "What's wrong?"

Only one reason could dim her enthusiasm. Warren.

"He had to approve everything," she said when Hunter joined her by the counter. "The food we ate, the shows we watched. I never would have been able to decorate."

"Abby—"

"You're not Warren. Don't worry, that lesson's been hammered home."

Soft fingers touched his cheek. Hunter felt their contact all the way to his toes. It was like velvet against sandpaper.

"Thank you," she said.

"For what?" He was distracted by the hand warming his skin. "Letting you hang pictures?"

"For trusting me. For not assuming I'll mess it up."

Never had someone's words hit him so hard. They gave birth to a sensation like nothing Hunter had ever felt before. A primal sensation that rose from somewhere deep inside him, filling his chest and fueling his protectiveness.

Just like that afternoon at the castle, everything disappeared from view but Abby's face. He felt as if he was falling, and grabbed the edge of the counter to stay balanced. His eyes dropped to her mouth. He wanted to kiss her again. But having pushed her away, he couldn't. Kissing her now would only confuse them both, and make him no better than her miserable, selfish ex.

"If you want to hang pictures, come with

me," he told her. "And bring a sweater. You're going to need it."

"Where are we going?"

"I'm going to show you something no other person has ever seen." With a small smile, he presented his offering. "My archives."

CHAPTER NINE

PULLING HER CARDIGAN tightly around her middle, Abby unlocked the door to Hunter's archives. He'd built the climate-controlled room in the basement of the building. The smell of cool, dead air drifted out the darkened doorway. As she flicked on the overhead light, bathing the space in fluorescent white light, Abby yet again marveled at the row of boxes organized by date and location. Alberta, Arcadia, Athens. People and events from around the world.

"You did this?" she'd asked the first time she saw the meticulous organization. "Impossible."

"What makes you say that?"

"You forget I clean your living room. This is way too orderly."

Hunter had pretended to be hurt. "I happened to have spent days creating this room."

When she'd responded with a sidelong look, he'd shrugged. "Supervisorally speaking."

He'd given her a tour, pointing out certain countries and projects he remembered fondly. "If you can't find a photograph or two in here to hang on my walls, you're in trouble. We're talking a lifetime of pictures."

"A lifetime, huh?" She'd pulled a box off a shelf at random. "Did you always know?" she asked. "What you wanted to be?"

He'd shrugged again, a more serious gesture than the first one. "I'm not sure. I think part of me did. God knows, I drove the Pomeranian crazy." Abby had smiled at the image.

"Mostly, though, I wanted to be like my dad. Then, what kid doesn't?"

"Me. My stepfather was a landscaper. I can safely say I never wanted to mow lawns."

"Point taken. *I* wanted to be my father, though. I guess I thought…"

Hunter had drifted off before finishing, both his voice and his presence. It had taken Abby touching his arm to bring him back. "You guessed what?"

"It would give us something in common. After my mom died, photography was the one thing we could talk about. Then, when I got older, he started taking me on his expeditions during the summer." There'd been a wistful note to Hunter's words when he said them.

"Father-son photo trips," she'd remarked.

"More like father-photo-son-set-up-lights trips. I worked on the crew, remember?"

"Must have been fun."

"I definitely learned a lot from watching him, that's for sure."

Twice he'd said he learned from watching his father. What about being with him? She had yet to hear Hunter say anything about sharing their passion. "He didn't teach you directly?"

She recalled Hunter fiddling with the metal label holder on one of the boxes, running his index finger around the corners. "My father," he'd told her in a voice quieter than she'd ever heard him use before, "taught me that in order to take great photos, you couldn't have distractions. That the best photos froze time at the exact right moment. He was famous for waiting for days to find that right moment."

"It's all about the shot," Abby had murmured, parroting the words he'd said to her.

Hunter's eyes became gray mist. "He did take some amazing shots."

But what about his son? Abby wondered. What did he do while his father focused on the all-important picture?

"You were lucky." Sensing a sadness about to descend on his shoulders, she'd decided to change the subject. "You had a passion. Only passion I had was wishing I lived somewhere else."

"Like Cinderella's castle?"

He'd remembered. "You saw how well that worked out," she'd pointed out. Looking back, the memory seemed childish and foolish. "Maybe if I'd had someone to warn me, life might have turned out differently."

"But then you might not have ended up here," Hunter had replied.

Somehow the matter-of-fact words still managed to make her breath catch. "No," she'd replied. "I wouldn't have."

They'd smiled at each other like a pair of shy children.

Back in the present, Abby ran her fingers across the perfectly aligned boxes. It had been a compliment, Hunter showing her this room. She didn't want to think about the significance of his compliment. Staying with him the past week already had her on edge. Adding speculation would drive her mad.

Funny, she'd thought the days of feeling on eggshells were over the day she'd left Warren, but no. Here she was, still unsteady and living on constant alert. At least this time it wasn't fear of an outburst keeping her on edge. Rather it was a fear of her own weaknesses. She worried she might misread a smile or a gesture, and tumble deeper into attraction than she already was.

Take the other day. Right before Hunter mentioned his archive room, he had been staring at her with an intensity that made her heart race. The pupils in his eyes had darkened until only a thin sliver of silver showed around the black. Coupled with the way his expression intensified, she'd been certain he was about to kiss her. Instead, he'd invited her down here.

Leaving her back on edge.

She found the box by accident. It had been pushed to the back of the uppermost shelf. If she hadn't been moving a pair of photo containers, she might have missed it.

Standing on tiptoes, she pulled the brown cardboard closer. While the other boxes were organized, this one had clearly been thrown together. A range of dates had been hastily scrawled across one side in faded red marker. Abby smiled. Hunter's early years. Realizing the treasure she held, she couldn't resist her curiosity. Who knew, maybe she'd find the Pomeranian.

She pulled off the lid to the smell of chemicals and age. Whereas the photos in other boxes were organized in crisp plastic sleeves, the ones in this box were tossed in haphazardly, without regard to size or subject. Abby smiled again. This was the Hunter she knew and loved. No, not loved, she quickly corrected. She was nowhere near love.

Flipping through, she discovered a time line of his photography career. There were pictures of the infamous Pomeranian, one of which she set aside. A photo of a handsome man in linen pants and a white cotton shirt unbuttoned to his navel. He was beating the contents of a stainless steel bowl. Abby smiled. *Reynaldo.* A woman lying on a chaise longue, head covered by a floral scarf. Abby's smile faded. *His mother.* From there the photos moved outward. Views from his window. Kids playing ball. A girl petting a dog.

And of course, more photos of his father. On location, in his office and behind the camera. So many photos of the man behind his camera. Photo after photo of a world without Hunter.

She almost missed the envelope at the bottom of the box. Manila and faded from time. As she undid the clasp, she felt the hairs rising on the back of her neck. The fact the contents were separate from the rest of the box suggested she was treading into extremely private territory. But Hunter had told her she had permission to look, hadn't he?

A collection of photographs spilled onto her lap, both color and black-and-white. A laugh burst out when she saw the top one. It was of a pudgy-cheeked little boy offering an ice cream cone to a dog. Hunter at his most giving. Hunter's mother must have found the idea funny as well, because she was in the background, a huge grin on her face. Lord, but she'd been beautiful, Abby realized.

Another shot showed Hunter and his father rolling on the grass in a park. Both of them were laughing, their heads thrown back, mouths wide-open with glee. And a third was a professional portrait of the whole family. Hunter the impatient toddler, with the proud parents looking on with love.

No, check that. Hunter's mother looked on with love. Joseph Smith's smile was for his wife. One of complete adoration.

With a sudden, sickening heaviness, the final piece of the Hunter Smith puzzle slid into place. These photos were *before*. Before Hunter's mother had passed, before Joseph Smith turned to his career. It all made sense now. Joseph's lesson to his son: keep your distance. Losing his wife had been Joseph's

Somalia. The moment he'd decided to bury his heart behind the lens of a camera.

Hunter had told Abby a good picture told a story. These did that and more. They showed a time before life had given way to solitude and separation. His father hadn't just focused on his career. He'd pulled away from his son, leaving him to be another observer in a crowd of observers.

No wonder Somalia had hit Hunter so hard. He'd found a community, a place—people— he'd cared about, and a terrorist had selfishly destroyed them all.

Her poor Hunter. Abby looked at a photograph by her knee. It was of his father, behind the lens as always. The window behind him showed the reflection of a child. A small boy, with a brown mop of curls, hiding behind his own camera. Abby suddenly found herself picturing a young Hunter following his father around the world, doing his best to emulate the man in order to spark a conversation.

A good photographer fades into the background. No wonder Hunter was so good at what he did. If she was right—and her gut told her she was—he'd been practicing fading into the background for most of his life. Staying on the sidelines. This room held thousands of photos, all taken from the sidelines.

Her heart wept. She felt a tear slipping down her cheek. They had something else common, she and Hunter. Loneliness really was a great equalizer. He chased the emotion away by hiding behind a camera; she ran away from it by heading toward Warren. They were two peas in a pod.

With newfound understanding, she placed the cover back on the box. If Hunter were present, she'd wrap him in her arms and tell him he didn't need to be lonely anymore. That she was here.

Thankfully, he was thousands of miles away, and she was safe from making a fool of herself.

"Is this centered?"

It was three days later, and Abby stood on a too-small step stool, trying to hang a framed shot of Belgian soccer players over Hunter's sofa. She lifted a corner before looking over her shoulder. "Is it?"

"Close enough," Carmella replied.

"I don't want 'close enough.' It needs to be exact."

"I'm going to go with yes, seeing as how you measured three times."

"I'll measure again." With a sigh, Abby set the frame on the sofa. "I thought you came over to help me?" she remarked, heading in search of her tape measure.

Her friend swiveled her stool back and forth. "I came over to say hey. You're the one who tried to put me to work."

"Key word *tried*. So far all you've done is drink our coffee."

Hunter's coffee. Abby corrected the slip in her head.

"That's all I'm going to do, too," her friend replied. "Why are you going so crazy, anyway? Will he really notice if the picture is half an inch to the left?"

You never know, thought Abby. "Doesn't matter. I'll know. Now come here and hold the tape level so I can mark the spot again."

"Man, you're being nitpicky." Despite the grumbling, Carmella did as she was asked.

"I just want everything to be perfect." Hunter trusted her, and it was important he see his trust was well placed. This could be her one opportunity to say thank-you for all he'd done for her.

There was another reason she was taking her task so seriously. Her visit to Hunter's archives had opened her eyes. She finally realized why his apartment had felt incomplete. The emptiness wasn't caused by lack of artwork or the echo of footsteps, but by the lack of personality. A home reflected the people who lived there. Hunter had created a residential limbo, because that was how he lived. That wasn't who he was, however. As she'd seen over the past few weeks, Hunter Smith was far more complex than a man who merely snapped pictures on the sideline, or a gorgeous action hero. He was funny, smart, heroic, charming. It was important for Abby to create an apartment that showed the world all of Hunter's many sides. Why it was important, she wasn't sure. A niggling, nagging voice in the back of her head kept trying to speak up. Warn her about something. She pushed it aside.

Carmella was giving her a dirty look. "Are you going to mark the wall or aren't you?" she asked.

"Why? You in a hurry to get somewhere?"

"Actually, yes. I'm going apartment hunting." Abby almost dropped her end of the tape. Looking left, she saw Carmella grinning. "Finally pulled some money together. I'm out of there by next month."

This time, Abby did let go, to free up her arms for hugging. There was a crackling noise as the metal tape hit the ground. "I'm so glad for you! You must be so happy."

"You don't know the half of it," Carmella

said, giving her a squeeze and a grin. "Then again, maybe you do. I never thought I'd scrape enough up. I thought I'd be stuck paying for being with Eddie the rest of my life."

"I know that feeling," Abby muttered, though, thank heaven, things had never escalated to the terrifying heights of Carmella and her husband's fights.

"Warren given you a hard time lately?"

"Not in the past week, though I'm not relaxing yet." He could be biding his time. "Warren is like a bad penny. Just when you think he's gone, he pops back up."

"Let's hope when he does, he'll pop up when your big bad bodyguard is around."

"Hunter is not my bodyguard, Mella, and you know it. He's my boss."

"A pretty darn protective boss, then," the woman muttered over her mug. The comment made Abby shiver. *Protective* reminded her too much of *possessive,* which she'd done, thank you very much. In her experience, no good ever came from either one.

"His mother raised him to be chivalrous. He's only doing what he's been taught," she told her friend.

"Whatever. I hope he and Warren meet up again. I'd like to see the big fat weenie get pounded."

Abby would prefer Warren never came by again. "What makes you think I can't protect myself?"

"If you could, you wouldn't have wound up in McKenzie." It was a point that, sadly, Abby couldn't argue.

"How is your boss, anyway?" Carmella asked.

"Don't know. I haven't talked with him in a couple days." Three, actually, but who was counting?

"I thought you guys did that daily video thing."

"We usually do, but he's in an area with very poor connections." She reached for the hammer while doing her best to sound nonchalant. "We probably won't get a chance to talk until he gets near a city."

"That's a bummer."

Yes. "I'll survive. We're talking a week tops." She refused to acknowledge aloud how long the past three days had felt. Without Hunter's lanky frame, the apartment was too empty and quiet. Surrounded by his belongings, she felt his absence keenly.

Worst part was the not knowing how he was doing. Every morning she scoured the headlines to make sure nothing had happened in that part of the world overnight. So far, she'd read about demonstrations, but nothing major. Thank goodness.

Her tense nerves were Hunter's fault. Every time she did talk with him, she made a point of reminding him to be safe. The warnings fell on deaf ears. He would wave them off with a obligatory "I will," then go off and do his thing, without concern for who might be home worrying.

"Ouch!" She hadn't been paying attention, and the hammer slammed down on her thumb.

"You okay?"

"Fine." Served her right for thinking like she was more than a housekeeper. As if he had a responsibility to her. Hunter didn't consider himself responsible to anyone. *Which is how you wanted things, remember?*

In fact, she should be glad circumstances hadn't switched. Maybe she should ask Hunter for some pointers on how to keep the world at arm's length. She seemed to be having a problem in that area....

Her cell phone rang. "Would you grab that? I want to run my finger under cold water."

"Speak of the devil," Carmella replied. "It's Hunter."

"What's he calling for?"

"Maybe he misses you."

More likely he'd forgotten a piece of equipment. An important piece, no doubt, for him to make the drive to where he could get service. Abandoning care for her swollen thumb, she scooped the phone from Carmella's fingers.

"What's up?"

"Abby Gray?" The voice on the other line was definitely not Hunter. "My name is Miles Bean. I'm a colleague of Hunter's."

Colleague. Hunter's. Abby's stomach clenched. She gripped the countertop to keep her knees from shaking. A few feet away, Carmella held herself rigid, studying her. Abby had the feeling it was because she'd grown pale.

"Yes, Mr. Bean," she asked. "What can I do for you?"

"I'm afraid there's been an accident."

CHAPTER TEN

TWENTY-SEVEN STEPS to the rental car counter, fifty-four steps round-trip. Abby had pacing down to a science. It felt as if that's all she'd done since getting Miles's phone call.

As she made the turn for another lap, her eyes shot to the Customs exit. Nothing. The plane had landed twenty minutes ago. What was taking so long?

Hunter was hurt. Miles's news replayed itself in her head. There was a protest that turned ugly. Hunter was taking photos. Somehow he'd ended up crossing paths with the wrong people, and they'd attacked him.

"Brutal" was how Miles described it. "Though Hunter was more bent up about his camera being damaged."

Of course he was. That camera was his life, wasn't that what he'd said? She looked around for something to kick, settling for the air in front of her. Hadn't she warned him before he left to stay safe? But no, he had to get his perfect shot. Like father, like son.

She spotted him. Ducking through the exit door, sling hugging his right arm to his body. Abby let out her breath. She'd never been so happy to see someone in her life. For the first time since Miles had called, her chest didn't feel as if it had a giant weight sitting on it.

"Before you say anything, the doctor said both breaks will heal perfectly," he said. "I'll only be laid up a couple months. Eight weeks tops."

"Only eight weeks? How lucky." Upon closer look, she could see why Miles had said his injuries looked "nasty." Along with a cut above his left brow, Hunter had a vicious black eye that spread close to his cheekbone.

There was a second bruise on his chin, less noticeable thanks to his stubble. Lightly, she ran her fingertips along his jaw, surveying the damage. "You're lucky to be alive, from what Miles said."

"Miles can be overdramatic. You should read his wire pieces." Hunter caught her hand and gently squeezed her fingers. "You were worried." It sounded more like a question than a statement, and Abby realized he was unsure. Keeping the world at arm's length had its consequences.

"Couldn't help myself," she replied. "I tend to freak out when I get emergency phone calls from strangers. I was afraid I'd be unemployed again." Not to mention scared to death he might be lying battered and bruised in a street somewhere.

Her attempt at sounding unaffected failed, and, smile fading, he leaned forward until their foreheads rested against one another.

"I'm sorry I scared you, sweetheart."

She closed her eyes and exhaled as much of the stress and fear as she could. "I didn't know what to think. Not after talking to Miles."

"I told you, Miles is dramatic."

Dramatic or not, he'd painted a pretty horrible picture. Listening to him describe the scene, she'd felt physically ill. "What happened?"

"Wrong place at the wrong time is all." That wasn't all. He'd been attacked, for crying out loud. Abby knew there had to be more to the story. She wouldn't press, though. At least not now.

They stood nuzzled together as the crowds filed past, until Abby felt the trembling. It was coming from her. Her body was shaking. Hunter must have noticed, because he wrapped his good arm around her shoulders and drew her closer.

"Shouldn't this be the other way around?" she asked. "Me comforting you?" Though even as she spoke she was burying her face against his jacket.

Hunter's hand rubbed up and down her spine. "You are comforting me," he told her. "You have no idea how much."

He buried his nose in her hair. She could have sworn she felt him press a kiss to the top of her head. "Absolutely no idea."

Hunter took a pain pill before they left the airport, and dozed in the backseat while the driver weaved in and out of New York traffic. A few feet away, safely strapped in her seat belt, Abby used the respite to study Hunter's bruised face. The tiniest of muscles twitched beneath his eye, betraying the tension otherwise hidden by his relaxed posture. Every so often his mouth would draw into a frown as well, the lines in his face growing more pronounced. Below the neck, his ever-present field jacket had a stain on the collar. Blood. The discovery made her own run cold. How close had she come to losing him?

All because of a stupid photograph. Brushing a hand through his curls, she silently cursed his father for making him believe nothing else mattered.

"Mmmm. That feels nice."

She smiled at the drowsiness in his voice. "Someone's feeling no pain," she teased.

"Feel great. It's good to be home."

"We're not home yet."

"S'I am." He nudged her hand with his head, like a cat seeking petting. Abby obliged him with another stroke. "Mmm," he purred. "Missed you."

That was the painkillers talking. However, having a mind of their own, her insides decided to flutter anyway.

Hunter's eyes blinked open. "You were really worried about me?" His voice might have been low and husky, but Abby heard the lonely little boy with a camera. The one whose photos touched her so deeply.

She stroked his cheek. "Someone has to," she told him.

"I'm glad it's you." He searched her face, his eyes so dark Abby felt like she might drown in the grayness. He was touching her, she realized. His fingers tracing a path up and down her arm, each stroke leaving a trail of warm goose bumps.

"You're so beautiful," he murmured.

She could feel the flush working its way

across her skin. He didn't mean it. If anything, he was reacting to his own stress by looking for a connection.

"I think your painkillers are making you loopy."

"Not so loopy," he replied in a voice so low she could feel the reverberations. His hand moved up to cup the back of her head, pulling her closer. "Not so loopy at all."

Then he kissed her. A slow, deep, lingering kiss that turned her inside out. Sighing into his mouth, Abby melted closer. She'd been thinking of his kiss ever since she kissed him in the wine bar, and while somewhere in the back of her mind she knew warning bells had to be going off, she chose not to listen. Yes, kissing Hunter in return was a bad idea. No doubt he would back off once he came to his senses. She didn't care. In fact, she was glad he had his emotional walls. It meant she could keep hers.

Hunter woke up on the sofa alone. He had a vague memory of climbing the stairs to his apartment with his arm wrapped around Abby's waist, and refusing to go any farther. Before that, they'd been in the Town Car and he'd been...

Kissing Abby. No way he could forget *that*.

He'd only thought about kissing her the entire flight. Amazing how getting jumped in the middle of the street could knock some sense into a man. Had he really told her he'd missed her? His skin grew damp as he thought of the chance he'd taken. He'd come back from Libya determined to stop pussyfooting around, and take what he wanted. It was the only way to deal with all these strange feelings haunting him.

Granted, the seduction wasn't quite how he'd envisioned it going. For one thing, in his fantasy, he wasn't doped up on painkillers, and was able to take the kiss a lot further… But he wasn't complaining. He'd simply have to kiss her again properly later on.

She'd been worried about him. That still boggled his mind. No one had worried about him since his mother died. He'd always soldiered on by himself. If bad things happened, he grabbed his camera and took photos, while his inner walls kept the emotion out. So he didn't know quite how to handle the idea that another person cared about him. But when he'd looked into Abby's eyes and seen the concern reflected there, a window had opened and light poured inside. For the first time, he'd felt what it was like to have a connection with someone. A real connection, far deeper than simple desire. Frightened the hell out him. But if getting the snot kicked out of him had taught him anything, it was that he needed to do something. Otherwise, Abby would continue rattling around in his thoughts, distracting him from his work and causing him trouble. So he'd kissed her, and miracle of miracles, she'd kissed him back twice as hard. If only the stupid painkillers hadn't kicked in.

A noise in the kitchen caught his attention. Abby was washing dishes in the sink. Seeing her with her hair hanging limp and curly in her face, and her sweater sleeves rolled to her elbows, he felt a new rush of desire. She was wearing the scarf he'd bought in Israel. The dark gold thread wasn't as warm a color as Abby's hair, but the shade was close, and in the right light, they almost matched. Had he bought the scarf for that reason? Wouldn't surprise him. Even that first week, Abby had occupied his thoughts.

She definitely dominated his thoughts this week, so much so that here he was, lying on a sofa with a broken arm. He fingered the cast through his T-shirt. *Wonder what she'd say if she knew the entire story?*

"I thought you were sleeping."

Returning his attention to the kitchen, he

discovered her wiping her hands with a towel. "Much more fun watching you work."

"Because housework is such a spectator sport."

"It is when done by the right person."

A magnificent flush colored her cheeks. The way she blushed so easily was one of the qualities he found so attractive. Her skin turned such a pure color. Made him want to kiss every inch to see what other shades he could bring to the surface.

Unfortunately, she insisted on staying across the living area. He couldn't very well kiss anything if she was thirty feet away.

Wincing as stiffness in his shoulder made its presence known, he sat upright and patted the sofa cushion. "Come here."

A nervous shadow passed over her. Regret over the kiss? God, he hoped not. "I can't. I have to work. This apartment doesn't clean itself, you know."

"It's all right. Your boss won't mind. I have an in with him." Hunter patted the sofa. "Come sit."

"Thought you said you liked watching me work?"

"I'd much rather look at you close up."

Though Abby rolled her eyes, she put down

her dish towel and came to sit on the nearby chair, posture perfect.

"You can sit closer." He motioned to the sofa next to him.

She shook her head. "This is good." Good if you were into sitting ten feet apart. "I don't want to hurt your arm."

"Unless you step on me, the bone should be fine."

"Just in case, I'll sit over here."

"Suit yourself." Ignoring the twinge of disappointment her answer caused, he moved on. "You decorated."

Instantly, her face brightened. "You noticed."

Of course he'd noticed. Although it took him a moment for the changes to register in his medicine-soaked brain. During his short absence she'd taken his "barren beige walls," as she'd described them, and turned his living room into a photo gallery. Reprints of various location shots hung on the walls, filling the room with color and action. She'd added a few other touches, as well. Curtains and a few vases. For the first time since he'd bought the place, the apartment looked like home.

Home. A word he thought he'd never use. Must be the day for new experiences and feelings. Tripoli was a far bigger eye-opener than he'd thought.

Abby was waiting for his verdict, he realized, as though he was delivering the most important statement in the world. To think his opinion yielded such power for her made the hair on the back of his neck start to rise. That was a warning signal, he decided. But for what, he wasn't sure.

"I like your photo choices," he told her. He looked over his shoulder at the Belgian footballers. Wasn't the perfect selection for the space, but it wasn't bad, either. "You have a decent eye."

He might have told her she was Da Vinci from her beaming smile. "Thanks. I was nervous hanging the darn thing."

So was it nerves regarding his reaction to the apartment that had her sitting miles away? "You needn't be. I told you I trusted your judgment."

"So you said, but…" Abby swiped the bangs from her face. How to explain something she wasn't sure about herself?

"Please don't compare me to Warren," Hunter told her.

"Okay, I won't." Pushing herself to her feet, she walked to the sink and poured a glass of water. "Nor will I mention this was the first apartment I ever decorated on my own." And he'd barely noticed until now.

She set the water in front of him, along with a plastic bottle of pills. "Here. Should be close to your next scheduled dose."

Probably. He couldn't tell the time, because his watch face had been smashed in the fight. No matter; he'd rather deal with the pain than fall asleep again. "I don't need them."

"But your arm?"

"Isn't as bad as people are acting."

While he was talking, Abby had been busying herself with wiping a water ring from the coffee table. Every time she bent over it, the proximity brought him a hint of her presence—a glimpse of skin between her scarf and sweater; her scent. The sweet smell of her skin was enough to ignite his need to touch her.

"Stay," he said to her. A simple request, but at the same time, one that carried so much weight. "Don't go back to your chair."

To his great relief, she understood his message and sat down. On the edge of the sofa, but at least closer than she had been.

"What changed?" she asked him. "You were very clear the afternoon we were at the castle."

She meant why had he kissed her? Hunter decided to answer her honestly. "I did. Actually, to be more accurate, I didn't change."

"I don't understand."

Neither did he, completely. "I couldn't stop thinking about you. Nothing I did to shake my attraction to you worked. When I saw you in the airport, I realized it was a waste of time, fighting what I really wanted. So I kissed you.

"And—" deciding it was time to take matters into his own hands, he slid over, closing the space between them "—based on your reaction, I'm guessing you want me, too."

Her blush was enough of an answer.

She was staring at her lap, thoughts unreadable. "Abby, look at me." He cupped her jaw, bringing her face in line with his. What he found was a pair of lips, and eyes that shone bright as stars. "You're so beautiful," he whispered.

"Don't…" She shook her head. "It's not necessary. I don't need a lot of compliments."

Maybe not need, but she deserved to hear she was special. The emotions that had taken up residence inside his walls grew stronger still. If she wouldn't take words, he'd find another way.

With that, he lowered his mouth to hers and poured every compliment he wanted to say to her into his kiss.

"I knew you'd get restless. How on earth are you going to survive two months of inactivity?" He hadn't made it two full days.

Hunter had dragged Abby out for a walk along the Greenway. "I can't help it if I like fresh air," he said. The night was unseasonably warm, more like midspring than midfall. Stars dotted the cloudless sky like a big, sequined blanket. Occasionally a cyclist or jogger would pass them, but mostly they had the road to themselves as they walked the Hudson's edge.

It was the perfect setting for lovers.

Lovers. Was that what she and Hunter were? They'd never quite defined what it was they were doing. Unable to say why, she found the term sat uneasily with her.

It certainly wasn't Hunter. As a lover, he was everything she'd expected him to be. Passionate, skillful, generous. Set the bar high for his partner. Maybe that was the problem. She wasn't sure she could match the standard set by the other women who'd visited his bed.

Or maybe it was the word *love* that upset

her. Lord knew, that particular word was a land mine for her.

Plus, they weren't lovers. *Lovers* implied permanency, commitment. They shared neither. They were simply two people enjoying each other's company.

"You are a million miles away," Hunter said as he pressed a kiss to her temple. "Where'd you go?"

"Just enjoying the view." The lie left her uncomfortable, but she didn't want to rock the boat on such a beautiful night. Funny how easily a person could slip into old patterns. "I love how black the water is."

The only patterns on the water were the columned reflection of streetlights.

"Mmm."

She wondered if he was wishing he'd brought the camera.

It was weird, not seeing him with the strap around his neck.

"Do you feel naked?" she asked him. "Without your third eye?"

"Interestingly, no. Would have been too much hassle with my arm in the cast, anyway."

"Really? You have no trouble doing other activities."

"That's because I'm more motivated in

those 'other activities,'" he replied. "Speaking of the word *naked*..."

"We weren't."

"Weren't we?"

He leaned down and kissed her. As always, the moment went from sweet to heady with a speed that left her breathless.

"I could kiss you forever," he whispered, before pressing another small, hard kiss on her lips.

All Abby could do was nod as his comment stilled her insides. Something about Hunter had changed over the past twenty-four hours. Maybe it was her imagination, but he seemed different. He was definitely more tactile, using every opportunity to kiss or touch. She chalked up that change to a sexual haze; she had the need to stay in physical contact with him, too.

If it was only the touching, she wouldn't think twice. But his whole manner had shifted. She could feel the change in Hunter's kisses, and in comments like this one. Romantic, tender gestures that left her off balance. Could it be, after years of Warren dysfunction, she simply didn't understand how real couples behaved?

But we aren't a couple! The protest screamed loudly in her brain. She clung to the fact like a life preserver. Knowing this…thing between them was temporary kept her grounded. It would be too easy to fall otherwise.

They'd resumed walking. After a few moments of silence, Hunter cleared his throat. "Our visit to Belvedere Castle the other week got me thinking."

"About what?"

"Besides our first kiss?"

There he went again, saying things that made her heart skip a beat. Abby shivered. Without saying a word, Hunter pulled her closer. "I was thinking it might be interesting to shoot some of Europe's castles."

"What about your other work? For *Newstime?*"

"I was thinking of cutting back on the hard-core news stuff for a little while."

"Because of what happened in Libya?" He never had told her what happened during the riot. "Do you feel like talking about it?"

"Nothing much to say. I doubt my version is nearly as interesting as Miles's."

No, but it would be *his* version, and Abby was willing to listen. After all the listening he'd done for her, she owed him.

"Anyway," he continued, completely dodging the conversation, "the pictorial I had in mind would be Europe's forgotten castles. The smaller ones that had gone to ruin."

"Crumpled fairy tales," Abby quipped.

Hunter looked in her direction. Since they were between streetlights, his expression was marred by shadows, although she suspected he was shooting her a disapproving look. "We need to work on your fairy tales," he said.

"I already have." Or wasn't he listening at Belvedere when she'd said she was over her princess fantasy? "Prince Charming turns out to be a jerk, Cinderella moves out and learns self-defense." Apparently she could add the castle falling into ruin, too. "A much more realistic version, if you ask me."

"What about the sequel?"

"What sequel?"

"The one where she meets a new prince and he whisks her off for a two month European vacation to check out castles?"

"I don't think…" She paused as Hunter's words caught up with her. "Wait a minute. Are you inviting me to go along with you? To Europe?"

"Why not?"

"I—" Abby was floored. "You're talking weeks."

"Couple of months, more likely."

Months? "I don't know what to say."

"Yes would be a good start."

"Y-yes."

He gave her shoulder a squeeze. "I can't wait to show you Europe, sweetheart. There are so many beautiful things and places."

He began listing the various cities he wanted to show her.

Any other woman would be thrilled to receive such an offer. Especially if offered by a man like Hunter.

All Abby could feel at the moment was fear.

It was starting. Listening to him tell her what they'd be doing, where they'd be going, she felt her control slipping away little by little. He was making plans for a future she hadn't agreed to. She'd never said she wanted Europe. "I don't have a passport."

Even the shadows couldn't mask his frown as he stepped back. No doubt he expected her to be bursting with excitement. "We can have one expedited. We can have one done practically overnight."

"Great." She forced a smile.

"There's this hotel in the French Alps with a view you won't believe." He paused to study her face before running a hand along her cheek. She couldn't help her tremor. "I'm thinking I might have to trap you in there and not let you out of the bed for days."

"Let?" Abby whispered.

"For days."

He meant the comment as playful; she knew as much. "You make it sound like I'm your personal property."

Eyes never leaving hers, he planted a kiss on the inside of her wrist. "Would belonging to me be that bad?" he breathed across her skin.

That's when she saw it. The desire glowing in his eyes. Brilliantly lit by the streetlamp, a possessive gleam in his gray-blue eyes that said *you're mine*.

It had been there all along, hadn't it? That's why she'd felt so unsettled. The light had been there all along. Damn him.

Worst of all, a thrill actually passed through her when she saw the gleam.

It was happening again, wasn't it? She was on the cusp of being swallowed up. The signs were all there. Her obsessive need to avoid mistakes in decorating his apartment, her fibbing to keep from rocking the boat. He now he wanted to whisk her off to Europe, and she, like an idiot, had almost agreed. Before long, she'd be completely under Hunter's spell, and then what? The bottom would fall out. He'd leave or she'd fail him like she did Warren and…

Dammit! Hunter had promised. She'd believed him when he said he had nothing to offer emotionally. That he couldn't give her a relationship. Then he went and looked at her like a man staring at his prized possession. As if he cared.

"I have to get out of here." She broke from his grasp, hoping to flag a cab before Hunter could stop her.

"What the hell is going on?" Naturally, he ran after her. "Why are you leaving?"

She fought against the tug on her heart his confusion caused. "I just have to get out of here. I have to go…."

Go where? She couldn't stay at his apartment anymore. She'd have to pack her things and head back to McKenzie House. So much for fresh start number two.

And where were all the taxis? This was New York, for goodness' sake. Weren't there supposed to be taxicabs everywhere? A flash of yellow appeared. She waved her arm, only to have the car speed by her, backseat occupied.

Hunter gripped her shoulder, forcing her to turn around. "Whatever's got you worked up, you need to tell me. I'm not going to let you run off without an explanation."

He was right. She owed him more, but couldn't find the right words to explain.

"It's going to Europe, isn't it? You don't want to go. Fine."

"It's more than Europe."

"More how?"

She sniffed back the moisture threatening her eyes. He looked so confused and worried, and maybe just a little bit hurt. In a flash, she was back in the archives and remembering the boy on the sidelines. Regret tore her in half.

The tears she'd sniffed away a moment early burned her eyes. "I made a terrible mistake," she whispered.

"A mistake?"

She saw the second he understood. The shutters closed over his eyes and he pulled inward. Gone was the tender man she'd made love to. "I see."

"I'm so sorry." She hated that she'd hurt him. Like his father, like Naxar. He'd let her in, and she was going to have to betray that gift. If only she could explain. "I never— That is, I can't..." She stopped while a pair of joggers ran by. "I told myself I wouldn't make the same mistakes I made with Warren."

"Warren. For crying out loud." Hunter jabbed his hand through his hair. "How many times do I have to remind you I'm not your ex?"

"I know." He was, though, in some ways far more dangerous. "Which is why it would be so easy to make you the center of my world."

"I don't understand."

"I lost myself with Warren. I became this weak-kneed woman I didn't recognize, all because I decided he was my Prince Charming. Except he wasn't, and when I got free I promised myself I wouldn't lose myself for anyone ever again. I would rather be alone."

"I see." He stared at the ground for a long minute before turning his eyes back on her. Just before they hardened, she caught a glimpse of the lonely little boy in their depths. "Just one question."

"What?"

"When are you going to stop letting Warren run your life?"

"Warren isn't running anything." Hunter should know. He'd gone to the courthouse with her.

"Could have fooled me. Everything you do goes back to him."

How dare he? "Did you not listen to what I was saying? This is about not making the same mistakes. Excuse me for being cautious."

"Cautious or afraid?" he asked.

Silence filled the widening gap between them. Afraid? Who did he think he was? What did he expect her to do? Ignore the lessons of her past?

If he didn't understand that, then there was nothing more for them to say. Abby folded her arms across her chest. "Goodbye, Hunter."

Rather than say anything, he raised his arm. Within seconds, a yellow cab pulled to the sidewalk. As he opened the door, the scent of his aftershave drifted past, stabbing her in the heart. She hoped she never smelled the wonderful woodsy scent again.

"I'll be out within the hour," she told him.

"Suit yourself." With a shrug, he shut the door, leaving her to drive away without him.

CHAPTER ELEVEN

"I THINK I'VE LOOKED at every low-wage job in the five boroughs." Abby flopped down in the faded Queen Anne chair. "Nothing. Not even a fast-food job." She either lacked qualifications or arrived after the job had been filled.

"Cheer up," Carmella told her. "It's only been three days."

Three whole days since she'd left Hunter standing on the sidewalk. Three days back living in McKenzie House, looking for work. She had a running bet with herself which would take longer: finding a job or getting rid of the ache in her chest that had been constant since she'd closed that cab door. Odds were in the job search's favor, and so far, she hadn't gotten a single nibble.

"Wait, there is one," she told Carmella. "Overnight shift cleaning crew in an animal testing lab."

"Sounds fun. I've got to go answer the bell. It's my day for door duty."

"Maybe I'll be able to bring us home a pet," Abby called after her friend. She was secretly rooting for the job; working nights might keep her from tossing and turning in her bed.

The restlessness came from her perverse habit of replaying their parting argument in her head every night. Correction: her parting argument. In her replay, she was laying out her reasons for ending their affair, while Hunter said hardly a word. Except, of course, for his parting ones. *Cautious or afraid?*

Why was it when she listened to her arguments, they didn't stick the way those three words did?

Carmella came back into the room. "You have a visitor."

He was the last person Abby expected to see. But there Hunter was, handsome as ever in his faded field jacket and sunglasses. Seeing him, she leaped to her feet. Her first instinct was to run up to him, but she caught herself in time.

"Hi."

He didn't return the greeting. Last time they saw each other, he'd worn a cool, shuttered expression. He wore the same expression today. It was obvious he found seeing her uncomfortable.

What did he want then?

"How's your arm?"

Ignoring her question, he pulled a manila envelope from his bag. "I came by to give you this. It's from our day at Belvedere Castle."

The day of their first kiss. How could she forget?

In the envelope she found an 8 x 10 photograph. He must have snapped it when she was rambling on about castles and fairy tales. In this shot, she had her face tilted as she gazed beyond the camera, her hair blowing about her face.

"You said you lost the other one."

This photo was nothing like the one she had lost. In the photos he'd taken outside the diner, she looked tired and put-upon. In this picture, her face was animated. She was *smiling.* And her eyes sparkled with a vitality she didn't realize she was capable of. She looked alive. Happy.

"Thank you." She had trouble getting the words out; her throat had a lump stuck inside. "This is—"

"I missed the shot."

Abby looked up. "What shot?"

"In Libya. The protest. I didn't get the picture. My entire career…" Whatever he was going to say faded off as he paced away from her. "It's all about the shot. That's what I was always taught. That nothing is as important."

"I remember." Like father, like son.

"The day of the protest, I moved to the far end of the square. That's where I was when I got jumped."

"I'm sorry. I didn't know." She'd known there was more to the story than he would admit. Although why he was telling her now, she wasn't sure.

"You don't understand." Pivoting, he paced back to her. "I moved because I wanted to get out of the way of the crowd."

"What?" Was he saying he chose to move on purpose? Why would he do that?

"Because getting the picture wasn't as important to me as coming back in one piece."

Hunter stopped and looked her in the face. "Apparently my housekeeper wanted me to stay safe."

He'd done it for her. The man who put his photos first, who believed in staying uninvolved and on the sidelines, had taken her advice. She didn't know what to say. Her heart was racing too fast for her to form coherent thoughts. If she'd heard right, he was saying that he…

She hated the skip in her pulse. The way her heart leaped to life. Why did he have to go and make things worse by unlocking feelings she so desperately needed to keep under control?

She knew he'd come back different from his last trip, but she'd attributed the change to his being attacked. She had no idea that the attack was actually a result of his change. A price he'd paid for putting someone else's desires first.

What a huge risk he took, this man who'd been taught by life to hold the world at arm's length. Allowing himself to care about another person again. To care about *her*...

And what did she do with this precious gift he risked giving her? Turned it away. In her lowest of lows, she'd never felt as despicable as she did right now.

Tears burned the back of her throat. "I'm so sorry," she whispered. There had never been a more inadequate set of words in all the English language.

Fingers caught her chin, forcing her to look him in the eye. Into blue-gray depths whose shutters couldn't block the pain and hurt in their depths. "Me, too."

Hunter brushed her jaw with his thumb. Abby shut her eyes at the feeling. So good.

So tender. She felt his body close to hers. His breath on her skin.

Then it was gone. As if she'd never felt it at all. When she opened her eyes, Hunter had left, the only trace of his visit the photograph in her hands.

Long after she heard the front door close, Abby stayed and stared at the picture. His admission—or rather, what he was implying—turned everything upside down. He'd chosen safety and her over his career. Chosen her. How could he care for someone like her? A baggage-laden mess too scared to accept his gift.

Thing was, all her previous arguments still held. She was still weighed down with baggage, with the same concerns. Hunter was too good for her. Too good to her. It would be so easy to make him the center of her universe.

Moisture began to pool at the corners of her eyes. A tear slipped out and trailed down her cheek. She wiped it away, remembering how Hunter had once done the same. He was right. She was afraid. Afraid to take the same risk he'd taken.

Ironic, really. That day at Belvedere Castle, Hunter had told her he couldn't have a relationship. How wrong he'd been. Turned out it was Abby who couldn't.

Hunter had been the one to risk his heart. Too bad she didn't deserve it.

Abby didn't think her week could get any worse. She was wrong, of course. Seemed as if she was wrong a lot lately.

It happened as she was walking home from another fruitless day of looking for work. Turned out the lab cleaning job was a no-go. She'd lost the position to a much more attractive woman who'd interviewed before her. It figured. Abby couldn't even get a job cleaning animal droppings. Maybe it was karma, punishing her for hurting Hunter.

She was so busy kicking herself, she didn't see him until it was too late.

Warren's bulky figure blocked her path. "I was hoping I'd run into you." His voice had that false conciliatory tone he liked to use.

"Hoping or waiting for me to show up?"

"You're always so dramatic." He sneered down at her. "I just want to talk."

Yeah, well, she remembered the last "talk" he wanted to have. It had ended with her almost being dragged into his car by her hair. "There's still a restraining order out. I had the temporary one renewed."

"There you go again. Why do you always have to turn everything into an issue?"

"I turn...?" Abby shook her head. Engaging him was only going to make matters worse. "It's been months since we broke up, Warren. I'm not making an issue out of anything. In fact, the only thing I'm doing is leaving."

She started back down the sidewalk. Fortunately, they were on a busy street. There were enough passersby that she could hopefully walk away without incident. When she got to the house, she'd call the police. They might not be able to do much, but they would at least pay Warren a visit and remind him to lay off.

"Where you going?" He grabbed her upper arm. Damn.

"Let go of me, Warren."

"I treated you good, and you know it." Like that, the mask slipped. He squeezed her arm a little tighter. "The problem is you never appreciated all the things I did for you. You were always ungrateful."

Just the opposite. She'd been too grateful, Abby realized. Convinced she didn't deserve better, and that was why she'd stayed as long as she had. But now she had experienced better. No way was she going back.

She looked long and hard at the man she'd once pinned her hopes and dreams on. Her

"Prince Charming." The second biggest regret of her life.

Huh. All this time, all this power she'd assigned him, and he'd dropped to *second*. A distant second at that. Losing Hunter, a man so above Warren in every conceivable way, was far, far worse. The realization made her laugh aloud.

"What's so funny?"

"You," she said. "I just realized how truly unimportant you are in my life. God, I wasted so much time."

Warren stepped closer, his eyes narrowing into an angry glare. "What's that supposed to mean?"

"It means…" Giving a hard yank, she broke free of his grasp. "It means I don't have to put up with you anymore. I put up with your abuse for way too long, but no more. Not ever. We're through. We've been through for a long, long time. I don't ever want to see you again."

He reached for her a second time, but expecting the movement, she stepped backward.

"Do. Not. Touch. Me. Again." She said the words with deliberate precision. Inside, her heart was racing a mile a minute; this standoff could end up backfiring. "We are over. If you come near me again, I will have the police on your behind so fast you won't be able to sit down for a month. Got it?"

"You're not serious."

"Try me." When he didn't move, she turned and walked up to the nearest pedestrian. "Excuse me, sir," she said in a voice loud enough for everyone on the sidewalk to hear. "Could you do me a favor? That man by the maroon sports car is my ex-boyfriend and he's violating the restraining order I took out on him. Would you mind being my witness while I call the police and have him reported? I'm afraid to stay alone for my personal safety."

The stranger, who happened to be a very large, very intimidating-looking man himself, glanced at Warren, then back to her. "Sure," he said, folding his arms across his expansive chest. "Be glad to." Abby gave a silent thank-you that her luck had finally started to turn.

"No need to call the cops," Warren said. "I'm leaving."

As Abby had known he would. Two things she could count on when it came to Warren: his mean streak and his sense of self-preservation.

"But when that fancy new boyfriend of yours dumps you, don't come crawling back. I don't do sloppy seconds."

Add a third thing. His need for the last

word. "Too late," she said as she watched his car drive away. "Hunter's already gone, and I'm still not coming back."

After making sure Warren had driven around the corner and out of her life for good, she finally let out the breath she'd been holding and thanked her Good Samaritan.

"Not a problem. I got a sister around the same age as you who had a boyfriend like that. Till she decided she deserved better."

"We all deserve better," Abby told him. For the first time in she didn't know how long, she truly believed those words. She *did* deserve better.

This, she realized, must be what empowerment felt like. She suddenly felt as if she could do anything, be anyone she wanted to be. Her mind flashed to the picture Hunter had taken at Belvedere Castle, and she smiled. She knew now who she wanted to be. And who she wanted to be with. First, though, she had some planning to do. Serious planning. She still didn't deserve Hunter. Not as the woman she was today. But maybe, with some hard work, she could become a woman who did.

Hopefully, when the transformation was complete, she could convince Hunter to let her have another chance. After all, when it came to second chances, third time had to be the charm.

Hunter hated waffles, but he ordered them anyway. Truth was he hated all the breakfast foods he'd eaten in the past three months. But he didn't want eggs. He'd lost his appetite for them.

He was sitting in Guy's Diner. As he'd told Abby, the scrawny little man wanted money more than he wanted to banish Hunter from his restaurant. New table, though. He didn't like sitting in the back anymore. And he didn't like the new waitress. She was too short and too brunette. He missed the color of butterscotch hair.

Abby. He breathed her name over the rim of his coffee. Beautiful, screwed-up Abby. But he'd finally learned his lesson. Photos were meant to be taken, not participated in. Next time he found himself drawn by his subject matter, he'd follow her example and run the other way.

It was getting increasingly hard to rebuild the walls around his heart, however. Three months and he was still struggling to feel numb again.

At least he'd had the cast taken off his arm. He'd already accepted an assignment.

A plate suddenly slid in front of him. He rolled his eyes. Just his luck, the new waitress not only got his order wrong, but had delivered eggs. Over easy, with a side of bacon and whole wheat.

Slowly he raised his eyes.

"So the thing with fairy tales… No one ever tells the princess that in order to get the castle and Prince Charming, she has to believe she deserves to live happily ever after."

Abby stood before him.

"Mind if I sit down?" she asked.

Before he could respond, she pulled out a chair. "You got your cast off," she said. "Good to see."

He couldn't do this. Whatever numbness he had managed to achieve threatened to crumble. To mask his pain he turned harsh. "What do you want, Abby? Or have you torn a page from your ex's book and taken up harassment?"

"No harassment, I promise. If you want me to leave, I will. Guy would have a fit if I caused another scene. Do you want me to go?"

Yes. It hurt too much for her to stay. "Up to you."

"I missed that shrug," she said. The waitress came by and Abby turned her cup over, signaling she wanted a coffee. Whatever the reason for her reappearance, she wasn't planning for it to be quick.

Hunter wasn't sure if her lingering was a good idea or not. Part of him wanted to hold her in the seat and keep her there forever. The other part wanted to tell her to go to hell.

Why was she here, anyway? His pulse picked up with hope. Damn, but he hated that he had hope.

She looked different. Hunter wasn't quite sure how. Her hair was still stubbornly independent. Today's topknot had already slid to the right and was half undone. Beneath her winter coat, she wore some kind of uniform, pink and institutional. It'd be boring except for... Was that...? Beneath the table, he squeezed his knee to remind himself this wasn't a dream. She was wearing the scarf he'd bought her in Libya.

She must have noticed what he was looking at, because she offered a shy smile. "I got a new job. At the Landmark. I'm a housekeeper. Who knew cleaning your place for a couple weeks would pay off?"

Even without his reference. "Good. I hoped you'd find work." It was true. He regretted what had happened between them, but he never wished that she'd do anything but land on her feet. "That's not what I was looking at, though."

"I know." Her cheeks turned pink to match the uniform. "I wear it every day."

"That's nice." He didn't dare think it meant anything more than a fashion accessory.

"You know why?"

"Because it matches your uniform."

She looked down, and smiled. "So it does. Honestly, I never paid attention. See, I don't wear it to be fashionable."

"Then why do you?"

While speaking, she'd picked up a sugar packet. Now she fidgeted with the little white square, flattening one end against the table, then the other. "As a reminder," she replied softly.

A reminder of what? Another set of mistakes to avoid?

Abby's palms were sweating. This was harder than she'd thought it would be. Then again, three months was a long time. What if he'd decided during that time that he'd been wrong? That he didn't care about her? What if she'd been wrong and his feelings weren't as deep as she thought? It was quite possible everything in her heart was one-sided.

She wished she'd thought to lay her new cell phone on the table so she could look at the lock screen. The photo of her at the castle was on it. As she did with the scarf around her neck, she used the picture to remind her of the woman she wanted to be. And the man she hoped to become worthy of.

As if seeing Hunter wasn't reminder enough of that goal. Time off hadn't been good to him. The ruddiness was gone from his skin; he was pale from spending too much time indoors.

He'd shed the field jacket, too, in favor of a battered leather bomber that had seen better days.

"Are you planning to answer?" he asked. "Or stare into space?"

Same old Hunter. "I didn't expect to see you here," she said, ignoring his question. "I came in for coffee and saw you sitting here."

"You happened to come into Guy's?"

"I was on my way to your apartment."

"Oh." He was doing his best to sound disinterested, but the crack in his voice betrayed him.

"I have to admit, I was afraid you might have left on assignment already."

"I leave in a couple of days."

At the news, her heart started to sink, but

she gave herself a mental kick. *What did you think he'd do? Stop working?* She would consider herself lucky she'd caught him when she did. "Where to?" she asked.

"Seychelles. Photographing the cinnamon harvest."

"Still laying off the protests?"

"Decided to start slow. What do you want, Abby? I thought we said everything we had to say three months ago."

Her answer was interrupted by the waitress, who set an order of waffles on the table. Abby looked at the plate.

"I'm taking a break from my usual," Hunter replied, shoving the plate Abby brought to the side.

"That why you aren't sitting in the corner?"

"I thought I'd try something different."

Both answers, for no logical reason, fueled her resolve. If he was avoiding his routine, perhaps it was because he was looking to forget?

"I made a few changes myself," she said, taking advantage of the opening. "I moved out of McKenzie House. Carmella and I got an apartment."

"Glad to hear you're back on your feet."

"Well, that is the point of a temporary shelter. Though I didn't completely leave. I'm volunteering there."

"You are."

"Three days a week. Leading a discussion group for women who were in the same place I was."

"You are?"

He was trying to hide the surprise in his voice. "It's okay. If I were in your shoes, I'd be skeptical, too. Like I told you, I've made a lot of changes."

Following her encounter with Warren, she'd done a lot of thinking about the paths she'd taken in life. Most of her decisions were because she'd been looking for someone to come save her, she realized. That's why she'd lost herself to Warren, why she'd been afraid she'd lose herself to Hunter—because she believed those men were her only hope at grasping the fairy tale. Once she'd figured out that responsibility, and success, lay with her, she'd started looking at her decisions in a new way.

"These women help me as much as I help them. We're learning we need to earn our happy ever after."

Hunter leaned forward. "You always said there needed to be a new version of the fairy tale."

She had his attention. "I did, didn't I?

By the way, when I say earn, I don't mean doing everything perfect. That's where I went wrong. Prince Charming doesn't expect you to make him the center of your universe, like Warren did.

"I know," she added, holding up a hand. "Most of the men in the world aren't Warren. I get that now. He's gone, by the way. Haven't heard a peep from him in three months."

"You must be relieved."

"I'm glad not to have to look over my shoulder." Otherwise, Warren was nothing but a bad-tasting memory. There was only one man that mattered, as far as she was concerned, and he was sitting at this table. While they were talking, the coolness in his eyes had changed. They'd grown bluer, more receptive.

Abby waited while he sipped his coffee and absorbed all she'd told him. She'd done a lot of work in the past three months. While it only the tip of the iceberg as far as the changes she wanted to make, she hoped she'd made enough headway that he might let her past the walls again.

Finally he set down his cup. "Congratulations. You're finally getting a second chance."

"Again. By all counts, this is my third second chance this year."

"Well, you know what they say, third time's the charm." He offered a smile. A small one, but more gorgeous than any Abby had seen in months.

Seizing the smile in her heart, she decided it was time to take the biggest leap of faith she'd ever attempted.

"There's something else I wanted to tell you." Sliding the breakfast plates aside, she laid her hand on the table, a breath away from touching him. It felt as if her heart was trying to beat its way out of her chest, her pulse was going so fast.

No one said laying yourself bare would be easy. "I love you."

Silence. Abby fought against the sinking sensation by reminding herself that saying those three words wouldn't fix everything. Hunter had been hurt, truly hurt. He needed time to accept that she meant what she said.

"You were right," she told him. "I was afraid of my feelings. Running from relationships was no different than running away from my parents' house with Warren. Only without the bruises. Bruises might have been easier. They didn't hurt nearly as badly as being apart from you did. Does."

Hunter stared at the Formica beneath their hands. When had he laid his hand on the table? Abby wondered. They were side-by-side, close enough that she could feel the heat.

"I don't know what to say. It's been three months."

So little time, but such a long time, too. "How about that you still have feelings for me?"

"I leave for the South Pacific in three days."

She'd waited too long. He wasn't able to let her past the walls anymore. Now she knew how Hunter had felt that night on the Greenway. Her chest seemed to have been stomped into a million pieces.

"Good thing I tracked you down when I did." No sense staying and making the awkwardness worse. She pushed away from the table and turned her head away. "I just wanted to make sure you know that when faced with a choice between security and you, I chose you."

"They tell me Seychelles is gorgeous this time of year."

Slowly she looked back at him. The vulnerability on Hunter's face took her breath away. Gone were the walls he'd hidden behind for so long. There was nothing but pure, open emotion.

"I've never been there before," he was saying. "Nothing I'd like better than to discover it with the woman I love."

He still loved her. Moreover, he was showing her by putting himself and his heart out there for the taking. To Abby, it was the bravest gesture she'd ever witnessed.

"There's nothing I'd like better than to go with you. But that's what I've been working on all these months. I don't want to make you the center of my world. I want to be the kind of woman who walks with you, by your side."

He cupped her cheek. Abby wondered if the shine she saw in his eyes was from tears. Hard to tell, since her own eyes were filled to the brim. "You always were that woman," he whispered. "You just needed to meet her for yourself."

"I have."

"I'm glad." He pulled her to his lap so fast she squealed. "This mean I should order a second plane ticket?"

Exploring a tropical island with the man she loved. Abby couldn't think of a more perfect ending to a fairy tale.

Which was why it killed her to give him her answer. "I'm sorry, Hunter, but no."

CHAPTER TWELVE

SEEING HUNTER'S FACE FALL, Abby rushed to explain. He'd taken such a chance himself; the words she said now would affect them both forever.

"It's not that I don't want to," she said. "I want nothing more than to run away with you." Doing so, however, would ruin all the work she'd done these past few months.

Plus there was another reason. "Please understand, I can't go. Not yet."

"Why not?"

"I have class. I started school," she added, seeing his confusion. "Remember when you asked me what I wanted to do with my life? I want to help women like me. Help other women get the power they need to rewrite their own life stories."

To her relief, she felt Hunter relax. "You found your passion."

"Oh, I found my passion, all right. Unfortunately, he's heading to the Seychelles to photograph cinnamon farms. Helping other women…that's what I want to do with my life, though.

"So," she said, lowering her forehead to his, "as much as I want to go with you—and believe me, I *so* want to go with you—I need to stay here. Do you understand?"

She held her breath. Changes and choices were all well and good, but the freefall moment where you learned the consequences were hell. Finally Hunter nodded. "After the way I lectured you, it'd be a little hypocritical if I didn't."

"No," Abby said with a watery smile, "it wouldn't. And I never said I wouldn't come for a visit. That is…"

Suddenly she felt shy and exposed. "That is, if you'd like," she finished, biting her lip.

"Oh, I'd like," Hunter replied. "I'd like very much."

His face was close to hers, warm and welcome. So welcome, Abby could barely breathe from the longing. And when his hand tangled in her curls, it felt as though she'd finally become whole.

"Very, very much," he whispered above her lips.

She kissed him with all the love in her

heart, telling him with her body what she'd already said with words. That she loved him. That she chose to be loved by him.

The abandon with which Hunter returned the kiss told her the same.

They broke apart, breathless and clinging, foreheads pressed together, neither ready to break the connection. "What happens when I get back?" Hunter asked.

The love she saw in his gaze almost made her want to change her mind about her plans and go to the Seychelles with him.

Almost.

"I'll have my apartment, you'll get a new assistant—preferably male, by the way—and we'll work on sharing each other's lives."

"I'd like that."

Abby's heart gave a happy jump. They'd both come a long way since that day he'd interrupted Warren. Somewhere along the way, Hunter had set down his camera and opened his arms to her, to include her in his world. And she…well, she'd found herself.

Happiness threatened to overwhelm her. Before the tears could come, she buried herself against Hunter's chest. Those strong arms that had once held her at her worst moment were here for the best.

His fingers combed her hair, making a bigger mess. She didn't care. She could stay like this forever.

"I've got one condition," she heard Hunter say.

Condition? Suddenly, her good feelings paused. "What condition?"

"That someday in the future I can ask for a merger. Your life, my life, one life."

"Oh, is that all?" She let out a breath. "I thought you were going to ask for something impossible."

"Does that mean you're amenable to my proposal?"

His proposal to propose? Absolutely. What's more, she knew that when that day came, and Hunter made that proposal a reality, she'd be ready, and she'd have the courage to say yes.

"Very amenable," she said, wrapping her arms around his neck. "Now, unless I misunderstood, we still have three days before you leave, and I have the afternoon off from work. Do you really want to spend our free time in Guy's Diner?"

"Sweetheart, Guy's Diner is the last place I want to be." After setting her on her feet, Hunter threw a wad of bills on the table and held out his hand. "How about I take you across the street so I can show you how much I missed you?"

"Now it's my turn to name a condition." She slipped her hand in his. "You have to let me show you back."

He grinned. "It's a deal."

Side by side, they walked out the door to whatever future life had in store. Abby didn't know where they were going or what they'd see, but so long as she had Hunter walking along next to her, she knew their ending would be a happy one.

* * * * *

LARGER-PRINT BOOKS!
GET 2 FREE LARGER-PRINT NOVELS PLUS
2 FREE GIFTS!

HARLEQUIN®

Romance

From the Heart, For the Heart

YES! Please send me 2 FREE LARGER-PRINT Harlequin® Romance novels and my 2 FREE gifts (gifts are worth about $10). After receiving them, if I don't wish to receive any more books, I can return the shipping statement marked "cancel." If I don't cancel, I will receive 4 brand-new novels every month and be billed just $4.84 per book in the U.S. or $5.24 per book in Canada. That's a savings of at least 19% off the cover price! It's quite a bargain! Shipping and handling is just 50¢ per book in the U.S. and 75¢ per book in Canada.* I understand that accepting the 2 free books and gifts places me under no obligation to buy anything. I can always return a shipment and cancel at any time. Even if I never buy another book, the two free books and gifts are mine to keep forever.

119/319 HDN F43Y

Name	(PLEASE PRINT)

Address	Apt. #

City	State/Prov.	Zip/Postal Code

Signature (if under 18, a parent or guardian must sign)

Mail to the **Harlequin® Reader Service:**
IN U.S.A.: P.O. Box 1867, Buffalo, NY 14240-1867
IN CANADA: P.O. Box 609, Fort Erie, Ontario L2A 5X3
Want to try two free books from another line?
Call 1-800-873-8635 or visit www.ReaderService.com.

* Terms and prices subject to change without notice. Prices do not include applicable taxes. Sales tax applicable in N.Y. Canadian residents will be charged applicable taxes. Offer not valid in Quebec. This offer is limited to one order per household. Not valid for current subscribers to Harlequin Romance Larger-Print books. All orders subject to credit approval. Credit or debit balances in a customer's account(s) may be offset by any other outstanding balance owed by or to the customer. Please allow 4 to 6 weeks for delivery. Offer available while quantities last.

Your Privacy—The Harlequin® Reader Service is committed to protecting your privacy. Our Privacy Policy is available online at www.ReaderService.com or upon request from the Harlequin Reader Service.

We make a portion of our mailing list available to reputable third parties that offer products we believe may interest you. If you prefer that we not exchange your name with third parties, or if you wish to clarify or modify your communication preferences, please visit us at www.ReaderService.com/consumerschoice or write to us at Harlequin Reader Service Preference Service, P.O. Box 9062, Buffalo, NY 14269. Include your complete name and address.

HRLP13R

*Next month, Kate Hardy brings you her heartwarming
new story, BOUND BY A BABY.*
*Emmy and Dylan are total opposites, so when they're
forced together to take care of their friend's baby, their
whole world is turned upside down!*

"Can we get this, as well? I think Tyler'd love it."

"You mean, *you* love it." Emmy seemed to like simple,
childlike things. And Dylan hadn't quite worked out yet
whether he found that more endearing or annoying. He
certainly didn't loathe her as much as he once had. She was
good with the baby, too.

Her eyes crinkled at the corners. "Okay, then, let's ask
him." She picked up the cot toy, crouched down beside the
pram, switched it on and let Tyler see the lights and hear the
lullaby.

Tyler's eyes went wide. Then he laughed and held his
hands out toward it.

Emmy looked up at him and smiled. "I think that's a yes."

Again a surge of attraction hit him. Was he crazy? This was
Emmy Jacobs, who sparred with him and sniped at him and
was his co-guardian. She was the last person he wanted to get
involved with. But at the same time he had to acknowledge
that there was something about her that really got under his
skin. Something that made him want to know more about her.
Get closer.

And that in itself was weird. He didn't do close. Never had.

HREXP0813

He didn't trust anyone to let them near enough.

The rest of the weekend turned out to be Dylan's first weekend of being a dad. Although it was officially Emmy's weekend on duty, he somehow ended up going to the park with her to take Tyler out for some fresh air. He noticed that she talked to Tyler all the time, even though there was no way a baby could possibly understand everything she said. She pointed out flowers and named the colors for him; she pointed out dogs and birds and squirrels.

She was clearly taking her duties as godmother and guardian really seriously, and Dylan was beginning to wonder just why he'd ever disliked her so much. Then again, this new Emmy didn't have a smart-aleck mouth. She didn't snipe, and she wasn't cynical and hard-bitten like the Emmy Jacobs he was used to.

Which one was the real Emmy? he wondered. Was she letting her guard down and letting him see the real her? Or was this just some kind of mirage and Spiky Emmy would return to drive him crazy?

BOUND BY A BABY by Kate Hardy
is available September 2013 only from
Harlequin Romance—don't miss it!